"I'm the most cold-hearted son-of-a-bitch you'll ever meet."

"Murder is not about lust and it's not about violence. It's about possession."

"We serial killers are your sons, we are your husbands, we are everywhere. And there will be more of your children dead tomorrow."

"You feel the last bit of breath leaving their body. You're looking into their eyes. A person in that situation is God!"

"You learn what you need to kill and take care of the details. It's like changing a tire. The first time you're careful. By the thirtieth time, you can't remember where you left the lug wrench."

"What's one less person on the face of the earth, anyway?"

~Ted Bundy - 1989

Tangle

With Tara

'TARA' SERIES
Detective Crime Mystery

About the Author

Jeri Lynn Stone lives in a small Arkansas town with her husband. She works at a large manufacturing plant in the Quality Assurance Department as an ISO Internal Auditor and Quality Assurance. Her and her husband love to camp and fish. They live in the center of four beautiful lakes and each are within twenty-five miles from home. They love going to antique car shows, gardening and Mother Nature. She has enjoyed writing novels, from historical to chick lit to mystery for about twelve years, now. She's currently working on the fourth novel in her Detective Crime Mystery "Tara" series.

BOOKS BY JERI LYNN STONE
'TARA' DETECTIVE CRIME MYSTERY SERIES
TAUNTING TARA
TEACHING TARA
TANGLE WITH TARA

COMING NEXT
TERRORIZING TARA

ACKNOWLEDGEMENT

I would like to thank my wonderful husband, my family, my husband's family, friends, and the wonderful writers' communities for the loving support they've given me all of these years. I'm very grateful and honored to have everyone in my life.
I would also like to thank my terrific critique partners. They keep me on the straight and narrow path in my writing career.
And, to my fans. You are the greatest. I appreciate you all.
I would like to give a special thanks to the law enforcement, first responders and all branches of the military for protecting us and our freedom. You have my deepest gratitude.

Thank you,
Jeri Lynn Stone

CHAPTER ONE

The young girls whimpered. Six of them cowered side by side, bound with quarter-inch chains secured to the wall, and looked at Detective Tara Woods with tormented eyes. Eyes that had seen the worst kind of hell, a nightmarish hell that would burn in their memories for the rest of their lives.

Tara whispered into the radio to her partner. "Dobbs, get your tail down here. I've found them." Thankful these girls hadn't met the same horrific fate of the two young bodies now laying in the morgue, she positioned her gun in front of her. She beamed her flashlight around the dark and dank basement that smelled of feces and stale air.

A large rat scampered across the dirty floor in front of her. She clamped a shaky hand over her mouth to keep from screaming. Damn, she hated rats almost as much as she hated sick bastards who preyed on young girls.

Dobbs gave the "all clear" signal and she relaxed. With all units hidden outside the mid-fifties style home, they would lay in wait until the sicko returned. And, she would do everything in her power to make sure he never hurt an innocent, again.

Tara turned back to face the poor girls and took the horrendous scene in further. Dirty, blue plastic dog bowls full of food scraps sat on the floor in front of each one. Evidently, the girls' lunch. She put on a glove and reached down to pick up one for forensic. Flies swarmed her hand. Her stomach churned. But, she'd seen much worse.

The bowl was still warm.

Warm? Her hand went to her gun.

With her flashlight beaming and her pistol drawn, her sharp gaze searched the deepest corners of the basement. Shadows bounced off the wall from the furnace and shelves, but no other soul was in the room other than her and the girls.

Damn it to hell, they had just missed him. How? She'd had men stationed around the neglected, two-story home thirty minutes before they'd entered the premises. There's no way he could've gotten past them.

She felt a chill run down her spine.

She turned to Dobbs as he came down the short, narrow stairs. "He's still here. The food's still warm. Just poured in."

Detective Matt Dobbs rubbed the stubble of blonde hair on his head. "Can't be. We searched the place top to bottom and every room. We came up empty."

"He's here. Search again."

Tara turned away knowing Dobbs trusted her instincts well enough to not question her. His shoes pounded back up the stairs as he shouted orders. They would search again. And, again if they had to before they captured him.

She replaced her pistol and knelt in front of the first girl, who didn't look to be more than twelve or thirteen. The girl shrank back as far as her chains allowed. She drew herself up into a tight ball. Her chest heaved with harsh breaths and sobs. Tears left curvy roads down her dirt-ridden cheeks.

"Honey, it's okay. Sh..., it's okay. I'm Detective Tara Woods. Everyone is safe now." God, she hoped she was telling the truth. Tara let her gaze follow the chain until she saw the padlock and cursed. She got on her radio and requested a heavy-duty chain cutter from her unit outside. Just a few more minutes and the girls would be free. She'd get them out of this hell hole.

"Can you tell me your name, honey?"

The young girl with dirty, matted, blonde hair and dark bruises showing through the rips in her tattered, bloody clothing nodded. Through swollen and cut lips, her voice raspy, she answered. "Sara."

Tara gripped the girl's trembling hand and smiled to sooth her fear. Sara, she remembered, was the first girl who'd gone missing six weeks earlier. Then, for each week afterwards, another had disappeared. Twelve-year-old Beth. Then Amy, Susan, Paige and now Toni. All in their early teens.

Fresh. Innocent. But, no longer.

And, no clues found to help their case.

Until, the lousy pervert made the biggest mistake of his sorry life when security cameras captured him watching little Toni ride her bicycle out of a convenience store parking lot not far from Tara's own apartment. The tape showed him approach Toni, and with a grown-up strength, he grabbed her by one arm. While she fought for her life, he pulled her into an older model, dark-blue van. Pitching the bike into the ditch by the roadside, he sped off into the night, out of sight.

No fingerprints except the child's were found on the bike. The camera's pictures were fuzzy, but they were able to get part of the New York license plate number. Melinda, their young and energetic computer guru, ran a match on the numbers which led them to a stolen vehicle. No surprise there.

Working with the local officers patrolling the areas where Toni and the other five girls were snatched, they realized that all of the victims lived within a five mile radius. Included in the radius were two unsolved murdered victims around the same age as the missing.

A little before midnight on Monday, the cops spotted the van parked on the street four miles away at this rundown address in a neighborhood where only crack heads, prostitutes and lowlifes lived. Tara and Dobbs made it there within minutes after they received the call.

Hearing a whimper, Tara turned her attention back to the girls as she waited for Dobbs to return. She wanted to scream. She wanted to make things right for them, to turn back time to when they were safe.

She wanted to kill.

Only the badge inside her pocket kept her from hunting the sick bastard down and putting a bullet between his eyes. But, he would pay his dues.

She would make certain of it.

The girls would need professional help later and for months and years to come, but for now, more importantly, they needed to believe they were safe from the monster who'd raped and abused them physically and mentally.

After a visit to the hospital the teens and their parents would be taken to the 13th precinct headquarters where the girls would be questioned while things were still fresh in their minds. They would finally be released to continue on with their wrecked life.

And then, their nightmares would begin.

CHAPTER TWO

Tara unlocked the door to her apartment and wearily stepped into her sanctuary. She closed the door with a soft click behind her and leaned heavily against the wood. It was 2 a.m. Tuesday morning. She was exhausted and pissed. The sorry perpetrator had climbed out an upstairs window and gotten away. Slipped right through their fingertips. She wouldn't rest until he was caught.

In her line of work, she'd seen too many cases like this and it never got any easier for her. Especially, the young. Each victim stole a little piece of her heart. She'd witnessed their pain, their numbness and their withdrawal from life and she knew from experience there wasn't a damn thing she could do to help ease the suffering.

Except, catch the bastard before he hurt or murdered, again.

Hearing footsteps, she jerked her head toward the kitchen. Jake, her sometimes live-in boyfriend stood leaning against the doorframe holding a cold beer out to her.

He was her eye candy.

His hard, chiseled face with a ready smile, straight black hair reaching his shoulders and a firm, athletic body with a dark tan and bedroom-blue eyes that seemed to look into her very soul was drool-worthy, drop dead gorgeous.

And, sexy.

Especially, when he wore nothing but a smile as he was now. He walked toward her, pulled her into his arms and kissed her long and hard.

They were both breathing heavy when he leaned back and held her beer out to her. "Long day?"

Tara took a long swallow and leaned against him. "Oh, yeah."

Jake nuzzled her neck. "Then, why don't I run you a hot bath before bed?"

She wrapped one leg around his hip. "Sounds heavenly. Will you join me?"

His wicked smile answered for him.

* * *

The phone shrilled from her bedside table, waking her from a deep sleep. With eyes still closed, Tara reached out and fumbled for her phone. 6.00 a.m. glowed on the bedside clock. Jake stirred beside her. He wrapped an arm around her waist and snuggled.

"Mm. Hello."

"Another girl's missing."

Tara jerked upward and sat on the side of the bed, brushing long, brown hair out of her eyes. "Talk to me, Dobbs"

The line went silent.

"Dobbs, are you still there?"

After a hesitant, silent moment, he cursed. "Yeah. You're not going to like this. It's Jenny Walker."

Tara's heart seemed to freeze in her body. She clenched the phone and shook her head in disbelief. "Oh God."

Jenny and her mom lived next door to her apartment building. During high school, Tara had babysat Jenny while Mrs. Walker worked. Tara had half raised the girl from diapers. Jenny had turned fourteen a month, ago.

Jake sat up and rubbed her arm in comfort.

She leaned back against him, needing his strength. "When was she taken?"

"The 911 call came through about fifteen minutes, ago. Tara, there's one other thing you need to know. The bastard left a note on her pillow."

Tara placed a clammy hand against her forehead. "What did ..., what did it say?"

Dobbs cleared his throat as if it pained him to speak. "It said in large typed bold letters, 'YOU CAN THANK DETECTIVE WOODS FOR THIS'."

* * *

Thirty minutes later after viewing the crime scene, Tara stood in Stacy's kitchen. Police officers, Dobbs and the crime lab were already outside working the kidnapping.

Tara poured two cups of coffee and sat down at the kitchen table and pushed one cup across to her friend. She clutched Stacy's quivering hand and studied her from across the table. Her friend's disheveled blonde hair and bath robe proved she hadn't been awake long. Her despair caused her to look ten years older. "Stacy, you know if you'd called me I would've been here sooner."

Distraught, with hot tears pouring down her face, Stacy used a tissue to dab her cheeks and nodded. "I know. I was so shocked and scared, I couldn't think. And, that note. Lord, I didn't know if you might be in danger, too. Or, why it said to blame you. I was so confused and I panicked. I'm sorry."

"No, I'm the one who should be sorry. I only hated you had to go through this by yourself. I'm here, now. But, I need to ask you a few questions. Do you think you're up to telling me how you found Jenny missing?" Tara patted her friends hand and picked up her cup. She sipped her coffee giving Stacy time to gather her thoughts.

Stacy inhaled a deep, shuddering breath and picked up her cup. Holding it in both hands, she brought it to her lips and took a sip. Placing the cup on the table, she ran one finger across the rim and spoke. "My head is still spinning from everything that's happened this morning, but I remember every detail. The alarm woke me up at 5:30, my usual time for a work day. I went to the kitchen to start the coffee and back up the stairs to wake Jenny. As soon as I walked into her room, I noticed a gentle breeze fluttered the curtains and I realized the window stood open." Stacy's eyes closed. Fresh tears flowed down her cheeks.

Tara leaned forward. Sympathy softened her words. "Stacy, I realize this is hard for you. But, I need to know everything. I can't help you or Jenny if you don't tell me what happened."

Stacy gripped her cup tighter and nodded. She glanced up at Tara. "Jenny never opens her window at night. You know how scared she used to be as a child of the boogie man? When she was around five years old, she heard a newscaster reporting about a child her age being kidnapped and taken out of the window. She's never forgotten about that child. And, having her father run off and leave us both when she was only four didn't help any, either."

Tara nodded. "She's had you. You've been a wonderful mother. I do remember having to check her window, under her bed and in her closet every night I babysat her. She wouldn't sleep until I assured her no one was there and they couldn't get to her."

"Well, she out grew believing something bad was under her bed or in her closet, but she still makes sure her window is closed and locked tight at night. And, when I saw the window open, I think my heart stopped. I started screaming her name and frantically searching her room. Her bed was empty, the sheets and bedspread were pulled off onto the floor. I ran from room to room searching for her, but she was nowhere to be found." Stacy's hand clutched her chest, her breathing intensified. Glancing up at Tara with fear in her eyes, she finished in a rush. "I went back to her bedroom and that's when I found the note on her dresser and called 911."

Before Tara could ask any more questions or comfort Stacy's fears, Dobbs entered the kitchen and caught her eye. "Woods, you've got to see this."

Excusing herself, Tara squeezed Stacy's shoulder as she passed. She followed Dobbs outside to the back of the house where Jenny's bedroom window was still open.

"Take a look at this. It was too dark outside to see earlier." Dobbs knelt down and pointed toward the ground where the crime investigators had placed fresh evidence markers.

Tara knelt beside him. Two small, side-by-side grooves had been plowed into the grass. She glanced at Dobbs. "He was dragging her. Those are heel marks. Jenny was struggling."

"That's what I thought. But, it doesn't fit his profile and we both know who we're dealing with. He's an evil bastard, but he's smart. Too smart to leave behind a trail and a note addressed to you to lead us to him. Too amateurish. Why wasn't he carrying her to eliminate any traces and why did he leave her conscious enough to dig in her heels and fight back? Something doesn't feel right about this."

"I agree, but, he has Jenny and with the note he left, I believe he's made this personal. That was his intention. He's been a busy man for the last few hours doing his research, and he knew the best way to punish me for breaking up his playhouse last night. Let's see where it leads us." She stood and began following the grooves across the back yard.

She lost the trail through the thicker grass areas, but picked it up again when they reached the graveled area behind their house. At some point, it looked like Jenny had struggled and planted her heels, using them as brakes, but then the uneven grooves would begin again as if she was once again unconscious. Or, much worse. Drops of blood appeared along the path in front of them. Tara cursed. Deep anger flowed through her.

She glanced at Dobbs. His jaw was clenched. "Let's catch the bastard," he told her.

"Believe me. It will be my pleasure."

TANGLE WITH TARA

About two hundred yards from the house, the yard turned into pavement. The other side of the road merged into woodland that surrounded a park a block down from her apartment.

Tall pine and large oak trees grew dense among the thick briars and vines not yet cleared by the park attendants. Tara's nose scrunched up. The smell of the musty, wet dirt from the soggy leaves layering the ground beneath the trees were pungent.

Glancing down, she realized the heel marks led right into the thick of the wooded area. Both Tara and Dobbs drew their pistols out before going any further.

Noticing a huge spider web woven between two pines, Tara frowned. "This is just frickin' great. Probably snakes in there, too."

Dobbs shook his head and grinned.

"What?"

"You're such a tough cop who puts the fear of God into dangerous criminals and yet, you squeak like a girl when you see rats, spiders or snakes. You amaze me, Woods."

Tara shot her partner, a thirty-year old, 6' 2", two hundred pounds, kickass, bad boy with blonde crew cut hair and green eyes, a dangerous look. "Hey, when I put this gun to a criminal's head, they know better than to frick with me. But, those varmints, they're not that smart. They'd bite me just for the hell of it."

Dobbs laughed. With one hand on her back he guided into the woods.

Twigs snapping beneath their feet made it impossible to move quietly. They walked slowly, following the heel marks down a jogging trail, zigzagging around the trees and bush and out of sight of the morning joggers. Too damn easy to follow.

It seemed like an eternity before Dobbs grabbed her arm and pointed. Tara drew in a sharp breath, but stood still until her eyes completely searched the area. Ahead of them, a wide circle had been cleared of all leaves and twigs. Jenny sat in the middle with her back against a large pine tree.

A large chain was wrapped a couple of times around her waist and the tree. Her hands were also bound and the chain was held together with a large lock. Her eyes were wide with fright and tears streamed steadily down her face.

A dog barked in the distance, but otherwise it was eerily silent. No squirrels chattered. No birds chirped from the trees above. Something frightened them. Her and Dobbs' presence? Maybe.

Seeing no immediate danger surrounding them, Tara gave their location and requested backup over the radio. She ran toward the girl confined to a tree and knelt beside her. "Jenny, honey. Are you okay?"

Eyes wide, her mouth taped, the girl nodded, her whole body trembling. Dried blood caked her dirty, blonde hair and grass-stained blue pajamas with pink hearts. Whispering reassurances, Tara began working on the chain and knew from the beginning it would be impossible to unlock. She reached for her radio and requested the backup to bring their tools to pick or break the lock.

While she talked she noticed Jenny jerking her head back and forth, her eyes widened and she stared behind Tara. A whimper escaped from behind the tape.

Dobbs screamed out, "Tara, behind you. Watch out."

As she twisted toward the sound of the scream, she heard a gun going off. She watched helplessly as Dobbs dropped to the forest floor, blood running down his arm.

Her knee hit the ground and her upper body swiveled around with her pistol held in front of her. Where was the bastard?

Then, she heard a twig snap behind her. Before she could glance toward the sound, a hard blow hit her head. She went down and out.

CHAPTER THREE

Something cold pressed against Tara's temple. She blinked her eyes against the throbbing pain pounding through her head and moaned. Hearing her name, she opened her eyes, one lid at a time.

Officer Jackson stood over her. A young paramedic knelt beside her holding a cold compress against a large goose egg on the side of her head. She tried to sit up when panic set in, but he held her down with a firm hand on her shoulder.

Frantic, she glanced around. "Dobbs? Jenny? Where are they, Jackson?"

Jackson's older knees cracked as he knelt down beside the paramedic. "Sh…, calm down. You may have a concussion. Dobbs is okay. Just a minor wound to his shoulder. He's being loaded into the ambulance as we speak. It's only for precaution. When they get back with the stretcher, they'll take you both to the hospital to check you out."

"What about Jenny?"

He sighed, looked away and stood.

"Jackson? What are you not telling me?"

His facial features screwed up in anger as he glanced down at her. "He took her. We're still searching the woods, but he had a good ten minutes lead."

Gritting her teeth and battling dizziness, she tried to sit up once more. "Jackson, I want you to take me back to headquarters."

"Tara. You need to listen to the paramedic and lie still. They're bringing the stretcher, now."

"I don't have time to go to the hospital. I have to find Jenny." Her stomach churned at the thought of Jenny, the child who meant so much to her was in the hands of that sadistic madman. Because of her job.

The paramedic shook his head. "Sorry, Detective. You won't be going anywhere except to the hospital. Hopefully you'll be released later today." He motioned for the stretcher. "Just lay back and we'll take care of you."

She thought about showing the young gun how well she was trained in Tae Kwan Do, but her head hurt like hell and she couldn't help Jenny if she passed out. She glanced up at Jackson, who shook his head. "He's right, Detective. I promise I'll turn over every leaf to find out which direction he took her. I'll have something to report when you get back from the hospital."

Knowing he was right, Tara relented. "Thank you, Jackson. I believe he's the same guy we were searching for last night. I doubt if he returned to the same house we raided last night, but check out the address, anyway."

"Will do."

The paramedics returned and lifted Tara onto the stretcher. Jackson patted her shoulder. "I'll keep you updated. You take care of yourself. You hear me, young lady?"

Tara grinned at his gruffness. "Yes, Dad. And, thank you."

* * *

Two hours later, Dobbs and Tara were both released with a prescription for pain pills and a warning to take it easy for a few days. Dobbs sported a white bandage on his right shoulder where the bullet only nicked the flesh. His arm was in a sling. The doctor told him he was lucky the bullet hadn't entered lower and hit a bone or an artery.

The swelling had gone down on Tara's temple, and she wasn't as dizzy or sick to her stomach as she had been earlier. She expected bruising later that would be hard to cover up. The light pain medication the on-duty nurse had administered earlier had eased her headache to a dull ache. The doctor had wanted to keep her overnight, but she'd refused. She had to find Jenny before the worst could happen. If it hadn't already.

Her gut clenched. The thought of facing Stacy with the news her only daughter was dead made her sick to her stomach. And, even more determined to find Jenny alive and well.

Jackson was there to pick them up when they were wheeled out of the hospital's electronic doors. He helped them into the cruiser, and cautioned Tara to hook her seatbelt. She gave him the evil eye behind his back even though she was growing fond of his fatherly gestures. She imagined her deceased father would've gave her the same words of caution. Jackson's obvious caring made her heart warm.

"What can you tell us, Jackson?" Smiling a thanks toward him, she settled back in the seat and leaned back against the headrest.

Dobbs slid into the backseat, and adjusted the sling. Disgruntled, he hooked his seat belt one-handed. "Just miss the pot holes, Jackson."

Jackson eased away from the entrance and pulled into the traffic. He looked back at Dobbs in the rearview mirror and grinned. "I'll try." Glancing at Tara, he responded to her question, "We found footprints and tire tracks next to the road on the south side of the wood line away from the jogging trail. Forensics is getting molds made from both. The tracks shows he was heading east, and you were right. He didn't go back to the house he was in last night."

Tara nodded, not a bit surprised. "He's a sick s.o.b., but he's not stupid. He knows exactly what he's doing."

Tara had no doubt he was behind Jenny's disappearance and the only way he could hurt her was by hurting Jenny. Hit close to home. And, that's what the monster had done.

Somehow he'd found out she was without family. Her parents had been murdered when she was only eight years old. Stacy, Jenny, Jake, Chief Haynes, Jackson and Dobbs were her family now.

So, he'd chosen the closest she had to a family and the most vulnerable. A young helpless teen, growing up and just developing. And, it gave her a sick feeling.

Dobbs stared out his window, deep in thought. "I agree. He's making a harsh statement. He's wanting us to back off, and as we said earlier, he wants to punish you."

Tara's heart lurched and then steeled. "By killing Jenny. Or worse. Make her wish she were dead."

"Exactly. But, we'll stop him before then." Dobbs leaned forward and squeezed her shoulder.

Tara shoved back her fears and nodded. "Yes, we will."

Jackson nodded, as well. "He doesn't know who he's messing with. He's tangling with the wrong person. You're a hellcat when you're riled."

A spurt of laughter erupted from Tara. Her mood lightened. "You're right, Jackson. Let's find this prick."

Dobbs chuckled from the back seat. He glanced out the window. "So, he was headed east. He could've hit the Interstate and be long gone by now, but, I don't think so. He'll want to watch your reactions, and he can't do that from a distance."

Tara agreed while keeping her eyes on their surroundings. "Hurting me and Jenny gives him pleasure. He'll stick around for the show."

"So, let's give him a show he'll remember while serving a full life sentence. But, for now he's going to be very disappointed when he doesn't see you cower or back down. If we could keep you and this case out of the media for a while he wouldn't be able to keep up with the investigation. He might get angry enough when his enjoyment is spoiled to make a major move to draw you out into the open."

"And, by doing so he could expose his own location. Or instead, it could make him angry enough to murder Jenny." Tara shook her head. "I can't take that chance, Dobbs."

"He would lose his leverage over you if he harmed Jenny and he knows it. He's enjoying playing the cat and mouse game with you."

"Until, he tires of the game." Tara glanced out the window. Her fingers rubbed her forehead to ease her dull headache and her worries. The last lingered heavy on her mind. She knew Dobbs' made a good point. You can't fight something you can't see or touch. Sighing, she nodded. "Let's do it."

Dobbs leaned over and rubbed her shoulder for reassurance. Without a word, he leaned back in his seat, pulled out his cell phone and dialed. It was picked up on the first ring. "Chief Haynes...yes, sir. We're fine. We were just released, but, we need your help. We'll explain when we come in, but right now we need all details of this case to be closed to the public and reporters." Dobbs listened. "Yes sir. I know they have the right, but we can promise to reveal everything to them soon, hopefully in a few hours. This could save the girl's life." He listened once more. "Thank you, Chief. We're heading back to the scene, now. Give us a couple of hours and we'll be back to headquarters and give you a full report."

* * *

Tara waved to her neighbor living a couple of blocks over walking his dog. She could set her clock by the appearance of him walking down her street at the same time every day.

Tara opened Stacy's door and walked in. The house appeared dead. No T.V. blaring. No music. No appliances humming loudly. Just silence.

Stacy sat at the kitchen table with a shredded tissue in her hand. Haunted eyes stared down at a cold cup of coffee. Her only daughter was missing.

Tara poured them both a fresh cup of coffee and sat across from her. Her heart went out to her friend.

Stacy looked up with red-rimmed eyes finally realizing she wasn't alone. She glanced around, her eyes fixated on the entrance to the kitchen. A tear slipped down her face. Her daughter wouldn't be coming through the door. Not now. And, maybe never. Her shoulders slumped. "You didn't find her."

Tara turned away finding it hard to face Stacy. "No. I'm sorry. You know I won't stop until I do. I promise you that. This is my fault and you have every right to hate me."

She stood and paced the floor. Dammit. Stacy's daughter was missing-or worse because of her.

All for revenge.

"Tara, I know you won't stop and I would never blame you. I know how much you care about Jenny. I wouldn't want any other team working to find her." Stacy stood and a comforting smile appeared. Her arms went around Tara and hugged her tight.

Tears clogged her throat. Stacy believing in her like a friend or a sister and not blaming her when she had every right to curse and scream at her meant everything to her. She gathered Stacy tight and hugged her back.

Before she could control her wobbly voice Dobbs came into the kitchen and walked over to stand next to her. Tara figured he'd waited outside until she and Stacy talked.

He gave them both a light squeeze and led them to the table. The three sat down before he spoke his thoughts. "I was thinking. He would've ditched his van by now. Gone back to his normal life."

Tara nodded. "I agree. I will guarantee you, without consulting a Behavior Analyst, he's a husband, father and probably employee of the month at his low paying job. A dedicated church member. No police record. His hands are squeaky clean on paper. A normal Joe who always flies under the radar. Unnoticeable in a crowd."

Dobbs nodded. "Maybe a blue collar who wears a uniform to blend in. I can't see him in a business suit or office where he has to be around a lot of professionals, but we can't overlook it, either."

"Do you know how many people would fit that description in New York? Thousands. You could be wasting precious time in finding Jenny." Stacy glanced at him with worry. She swirled her empty cup round and around on the table top. Her hands shook.

Tara gently squeezed Stacy's hand to stop the movement. "Don't worry. We have other people at the precinct who can search for us. Dobbs and I will still concentrate on finding Jenny. So, let's knock the uniform theory out of the equation first. Okay? I can't stand not doing anything. This is a good start." She stood and rounded the table to give her friend a hug. "Stacy, we'll be back soon."

Panic flared in Stacy's eyes. She clutched Tara's shirt sleeve. "What if he comes back? He may not be through hurting you."

Tara knelt beside her chair and looked her directly in the eye. "There are two officers outside tagging evidence. Scream out and they'll be here in seconds. I need to look for Jenny."

Tears rolled down the mother's face. "Bring her home to me."

"I promise. I will." Tara hugged her friend once more and stood with a renewed determination. She faced Dobbs. "Let's find Jackson. We need a ride to headquarters."

CHAPTER FOUR

Chief Haynes shuffled papers on his desk, scribbled his signature on several sheets of official documents while listening to Tara and Dobbs. When they finished explaining what they needed, he finally glanced up and laid his pen on the desk.

Rubbing his forehead, the Chief leaned back. "You have another teenage girl missing who can possibly be linked to the murder of two other girls found in the last two weeks. Plus, the abduction of the other six you rescued last night. I can only hold off the media for a few hours before they start screaming for a statement of some kind."

"We'll need more than a few hours, Chief," Dobbs said. "We don't know who we're dealing with now. We only have a grainy picture off that camera to show us what he looks like. We can ask the T.V. stations to run it for us. Someone might recognize him and pacify the media for a while without mentioning Jenny."

Tara glanced down at her hands, then back up to Chief Haynes who still looked hesitant. "Chief, we're talking about Jenny. You've met her. She's not a stranger to us. She's like a niece to me. Family. You know what family means to me." She felt Dobb's hand on her shoulder, just a light squeeze with his fingers, but enough to show his support.

Chief Haynes sighed, removed his reading glasses and rubbed his eyes. He glanced down at his watch. "It's ten o'clock. You have until in the morning before I call a press meeting."

Only Tara could get away with walking up to Chief Haynes behind closed doors and kissing him on the cheek. "Thank you, Sir."

Chief Haynes blushed to his roots. "Get out of here you two, and ...bring Jenny home safely."

"Yes. Sir. Thank you, Sir." Tara and Dobbs left the Chief's office pumped up and ready to stop a monster.

* * *

Jenny woke with a start, her heart racing and her mind blurred from whatever drug she'd been given to knock her out.

This was an awful nightmare, she thought. Just only, a nightmare.

She raised her head and opened her eyes hoping she was wrong, hoping to see her teenage bedroom with her favorite posters of her music teen idols hanging on the walls, calming and safe, a familiar bed with herself snuggled deep beneath the comforter. Her mother would be down the hall.

Instead, she saw nothing through the dingy back window of the moving van but power poles going by at a slow pace. It was daylight. The open fields, a few barns and houses in between with cattle grazing inside barbed wire fences were all unfamiliar to her. She didn't recognize any of these places.

The van's tire hit a pothole and she bounced against the hard floor and cried out. The tight chains on her wrists and feet clanged together and dug into her skin. Tears burned her eyes, but she refused to let them fall. He did remove the tape across her mouth and she could breathe, normal.

She looked down at her dirty and torn pajamas. Her nails and feet were bloody from her struggle. And, the worst... she remembered putting her cell phone on her night stand before climbing into bed.

Then, the van slowed and stopped. The motor died. Her world turned silent.

Oh god, she thought. The nightmare was real.

And, she was truly on her own.

* * *

Around 10:30 a.m., Dobbs returned from their computer analyst/guru, Melinda Cass's office. While he and Tara waited on the officers to report back on any information the closest neighbors to the house they'd raided last night could give them, they focused on the uniform theory.

Thinking the guy wouldn't deviate from his normal routine, Dobbs hoped someone noticed the kidnapper arriving or leaving the house. If so, maybe they could tell them which direction he headed and if he wore any type of uniform.

In the meantime, he'd started Melinda searching for all of the uniform suppliers and cleaners in and around New York City and their customers. If they had to, they would question and rule out each person wearing a uniform, starting with the two manufacturing plants located within a few miles from where he'd kidnapped his victims.

Then, there were the many restaurant workers, delivery services and utility workers to check out. Melinda promised the long list within a few hours. The search would be time consuming and would require using several officers, but could pay off big time. Or, they could come up empty handed. He prayed the neighbors came through on this.

Dobbs stuck his head in Tara's office to update her on his progress with Melinda only to find she wasn't there. He found her moments later downstairs in the Police Department's crude gym. An assortment of exercise equipment covered the floor mats. Wooden benches lined one wall with a door that led off to the showers and lockers.

Tara stood in the middle of the gym attacking the punching ball like it was a perp's face. Each angry punch pummeled the ball with renewed vigor. Right fist. Left fist. Back and forth while she rocked on the balls of her feet. A whoosh of breath left her lungs with each punch.

Her hair was pulled back into a short ponytail. Her white T-shirt and black work-out shorts clung damply to her sweaty skin. Her cheeks were red from exertion, but it was her fiery eyes that had Dobbs studying his partner as she unleashed her anger, fighting her own demons.

Finally, she stopped and hung her head to her chest as she regained her erratic breathing. He stepped into her line of vision and sat down on a bench near her. "You want to talk about it?"

Tara grabbed a towel and wiped the sweat off of her face. She snarled, "I don't need to be psychoanalyzed, Dobbs. I'm just pissed. It's better I beat the crap out of the ball rather than the perverts face when we catch him. But, I can't guarantee anything.

Dobbs looked down at his hands and spoke softly. "You're too close to this case, Tara. Jenny and Stacy are your friends. Plus, we're dealing with young, innocent girls." He looked up and met her angry gaze. "I saw your face in the basement last night. Those battered girls wrung your heart out, and I can only imagine how much you related to them. You were also a young victim when your parents were killed, and no matter how much you may say differently, you've never fully gotten over it. Both the Chief and I would understand if you worked on another case. This has to be messing with your mind and your heart, and it might cause you to make a mistake that could turn deadly for you or me."

Tara flung the towel down onto the bench next to Dobbs. She glanced at him with a stone coldness he'd only seen her show when facing down the bad guys. "I'm a professional, Dobbs. I wouldn't let that happen. The only thing that will stop me from catching this bastard is if I'm buried six feet under. You or the Chief may not agree with it, but don't try to stop me." She grabbed her gym bag and headed for the shower. Anger vibrated through her with each step.

Dobbs knew her anger wasn't directed toward him, but it was still lethal if she didn't get her head straight. She had to distance herself from the victim. She had to treat it as any other case. He sighed and stood up. His gut told him she would always conduct herself professionally. She would never put herself, him or Jenny in danger. But, he'd been her partner for enough years to recognize the battle warring inside her.

Good against evil.

Right from wrong.
An eye for an eye.
Which road would she take?

* * *

Tara stood beneath the shower until the soothing water turned cool and her anger subsided a little. The heavy guilt still burned inside her. She couldn't push past the fact Jenny was in danger because of her own inability to catch the bastard who kidnapped, murdered, and raped young, innocent girls.

She turned the water off and leaned her aching head against the shower stall. She knew Dobbs was right and he cared enough about her to tell her what he thought. She agreed that she was too close to the victim, but there was no way she was quitting the case. She needed to get her head back on straight and catch the pervert kidnapping and murdering these young girls. Before he murdered Jenny.

* * *

Thirty minutes later, dressed and carrying a greasy sack of hamburgers and fries along with a couple of soft drinks, Tara entered her partner's office. She set the sack and drinks on his desk and waited until he glanced up from his computer. "I've come bringing a peace offering, Oh Wise Man."

Dobbs sat back in his seat and laid his uninjured arm over his chest. "Wise man? I like that."

Tara noticed the grin he was trying so hard to hide. She continued. "I'm sorry for taking my frustrations out on you."

"No problem. If that's what I think it is in the bag, apology accepted."

"It is. And,...."

Her stomach grumbled. She sat on the edge of his desk and opened the sack. Pulling out a large fry, she shoved the sack toward Dobbs before stuffing the greasy potato slice into her mouth. She moaned in ecstasy. It was a good thing she'd worked out this evening. One hamburger might not be enough.

Dobbs took a bite of his burger and waved his hand in the air for her to continue. "You were saying?"

Tara licked the grease off her lips and watched Dobbs' eyes narrow. The dimple in his chin dipped deeper and his grin turned wicked. She did it, again. Slowly this time, knowing it was all in fun.

"Tara."

The warning in his voice had her laughing and hopping off his desk. With Jake in her life, Dobbs would always remain her partner in crime, her career brother. But damn, she loved torturing him every chance she got. Knowing he felt the same way and would eventually pay her back made it even more enjoyable.

She grabbed her container of fries before sitting in the chair across from him, out of his reach. She continued their conversation. "Look Dobbs. I know you're worried about me, but I promise I'll treat this case like any other."

Dobbs took a sip from his soft drink and studied her. He shook his head. "I believe you'll try."

"I won't just try. I'll do it. I'm okay, Dobbs. Really. I can't believe we're even having this stupid conversation. You know I'm capable of doing my job without partiality. And, to be honest, this isn't your decision to make." Tara told him.

Dobbs leaned forward and held her gaze. "It's my decision whether or not to work with someone who is highly volatile."

"I am not volatile. I can handle this. With or without you. And, that better not be sympathy I see in your eyes." She growled and moved to stand.

"Tara." His voice softened to almost a whisper. "No sympathy. I swear. You know I'll always be by your side. Just promise me you'll get help if this affects you any further. Everyone needs help sometimes. Even you."

Relenting and grateful for his words of support, she nodded. "I promise, but I won't need to see a psychiatrist, Dobbs. My mind is working just fine."

A reluctant smile appeared. "Tara, your mind has never worked just fine."

"Bite me, Dobbs." She grinned and with a seductive wink, licked her lips before walking out with a swing to her hips.

CHAPTER FIVE

Early evening, Albert Jones pulled into the gas station, grumbling about the lower gas mileage his other van used compared to this one. He cursed Detective Woods for forcing him into trading in his cheap, reliable vehicle. She was costing him money he couldn't afford or be accountable for. Too many questions from his wife and neighbors. Just another grievance he had against the Detective. She would pay.

Oh, yeah. She would pay.

He rubbed the dark, day-old bristles on his face and glanced in the rearview mirror at the girl in the back of the van. She was still knocked out. Good. Stepping out of the van, he pulled his worn blue jeans up around his waist and glanced around, checking out his surroundings before he began filling up his tank. An elderly man was filling up his car in the bay beside him. Albert turned his back on the man to keep his face hidden. No need for unnecessary attention.

Not seeing anyone else near the station, his thoughts turned to Mary, his sweet wife of seventeen years. She'd called him earlier, asking him to stop on his way home to pick up a gallon of milk. Timmy, their fourteen-year-old son was a growing boy. Albert grinned. That boy's stomach was a bottomless pit. He was never full.

TANGLE WITH TARA

Albert was coaching Timmy's summer baseball game later this evening. Other than his secret stash of girls, watching his son pitch was one of the highlights of his life. That boy could throw a hard curve ball as well as a professional. Or, maybe he was just a proud papa. He wouldn't miss tonight for the world.

But, first he had to unload his precious cargo. He didn't have far to drive, but the hours were ticking away.

The gas pump cut off and he replaced the nozzle. Screwing on the gas tank lid, he glanced through his tinted back cargo window to check out his latest possession and froze. The girl had crawled forward to the back seat, her back to the passenger door. With her hands tied behind her, she had one finger on the button to lower the window. She turned to the window and he saw from her reflection that she was mouthing for help to the older man parked beside them.

Albert watched the man's shocked face as he walked with hesitant steps closer to the van. The stranger's attention was on the girl.

Albert cursed his luck. He knew he should've left the tape over her mouth, but he feared she would awaken and lift herself up high enough for someone to see her mouth covered through the window.

In a swift motion, he reached inside his shirt, pulled out his 9mm pistol with a silencer attached and shot the man point blank in the center of his forehead. Not chancing another second in case one of the other customers inside the store had seen what happened, Albert climbed into the driver's seat, started the van, rolling up the window as he sped off.

Miles down the road, he pulled onto a familiar gravel road and hid the van behind an old abandoned house. Screaming, furious, he jumped out of the van, ran to the back, flung open the cargo door and climbed in. Grabbing her hair, he drug her back to the cargo space and pushed her hard to the floor.

"No. No. Nooooooooooooooo. Please, don't hurt me. I promise I won't do it, again." Sobs racked her body. She tried to scoot away.

"Bitch. I'll kill you if you ever try it, again. You saw what happened to the old man, didn't you? Didn't you?" He screamed. Grabbing her hair, he backhanded her. She fell to her side, blood running down her chin from a cut lip.

Reaching into his bag, he pulled out a syringe and a vial. Quickly filling the syringe with the highest dosage, he stuck the needle into the girl's arm. Within seconds, she was unconscious and looking like the little angel that increased his lustful thoughts. But, that would have to come later.

Climbing back out of the van, he paced back and forth on the side of the road, cursing and shaking. He had to think.

He slapped his forehead. Think.

What would he do now? Had someone gotten his license plates? Did they get a good look at him? Were there cameras at the station? Of course there were. Damn it. He would have to unload his cargo until he could steal another van. And, that would take time. He would miss his son's game.

* * *

TANGLE WITH TARA

Tara and Dobbs got the call. A man had been fatally shot at a convenience store a few miles away.

His wife witnessed it all.

Minutes later, Tara and Dobbs entered the store. She recognized the responding officer who sat beside an elderly lady taking notes.

The woman was systematically shredding a tissue while she answered Duncan's question. Tears choked her voice at first, but then she straightened her spine and continued with determined grit. "My husband was trying to help that poor girl, and that vile man pulled out a gun and just shot him. He killed my husband and it's my fault. I'm the one who wanted to go visit our kids in Atlanta this week. If it wasn't for me, we wouldn't have stopped to fill up. Oh, James. I'm so sorry. So sorry." The lady covered her face with her hands and gave in to her sorrow, her body shaking with her sobs.

Tara stepped forward and knelt beside Duncan, thankful he had taken the elderly woman to the office where she couldn't see her husband or the crime scene crew still working the scene. Tara wrapped her arms around the woman while the woman cried herself out. Finally, she quieted and looked up at Tara with blood-red eyes.

Duncan nodded toward her and Dobbs. "This is Mrs. Booker. Mrs. Booker, this is Detective Woods and Detective Dobbs, the homicide detectives who will be working your husband's case."

Dobbs handed the grieving woman another tissue. "Mrs. Booker, we're sorry about your husband. Can you tell us what happened?"

"James was filling the tank and I heard him say something. When I glanced out the driver's window from the passenger side he was walking toward the van next to us. I saw a young girl with her face against the window. She was mouthing, "HELP ME". She seemed so desperate. I noticed the man filling the van's tank look toward my husband in shock and then fear, maybe. He reached into his shirt and before I could comprehend what was happening or yell out a warning, he pulled out a gun and shot James. I never heard the shot. Then, the man jumped into the van and took off. By the time I got to my husband, someone from inside the store was beside me calling 911."

Tara gave a brief glance toward Dobbs. He looked back at her with a raised brow. Were they thinking the same thing? Could this be their man and was the young girl held captive in the van, Jenny? Were they lucky enough to finally get the lead they desperately needed? God, she hoped so. Her nerves jumped.

"Can you describe the man?" Tara asked.

Mrs. Booker gave a brief nod and sniffled. "Oh, yes. His image is burned into my brain. My husband was around five-foot-nine, so I'd say the man was maybe six-one or two. Probably weighed around two hundred pounds or so. Black hair, balding a little on the top, wearing round, black-rimmed glasses. Eyes so blue they reminded me of my glass cleaner at home. He had on some kind of white uniform type shirt with either his name or the name of the business embroidered on it. Sorry, everything happened so fast. I'm afraid that's all I remember."

Tara reached out and clutched Mrs. Booker's hands shredding a new tissue. She shot Dobbs a wide grin. Bingo. Now, they had a description to broadcast to all units. "That's a big help, Mrs. Booker. What about the van? Do you remember what model or color or maybe see the license plate?"

"No, I'm not any good with makes or models. It was an older, dark blue van, if that helps. It was bigger than the newer S.U.V's they're coming out with now. And, no I didn't see the plate. I was running toward James and didn't think to look. Maybe the guy who called 911 got a better look. You can ask him. I'm sorry for not being more help. And I do want to help you catch my husband's murderer." Her chin quivered. She looked like she'd aged twenty years in the last twenty minutes.

"You're doing great. Now, Mrs. Booker can you tell me anything about the young girl you saw inside the van. You said she was asking for help?" Tara's nails bit into her palms.

"Yes. She had her face pressed against the window. She kept glancing from the man and back to my husband like she was frightened the man would catch her. Her face was scratched, and it looked like she was wearing pajamas. Blue with pink hearts all over the top. Oh. And, her blonde hair was all tangled like it hadn't been brushed in days."

Tara jerked her head up toward Dobbs, her heart racing. "Jenny."

CHAPTER SIX

Tara rubbed her tired eyes and leaned back against the headrest. The guy who called 911 didn't get the license plate number like she'd hoped. He'd walked out of the store and saw the man falling. He thought the elderly man was having a heart attack at first until he saw the blood and heard the squeal of tires on the pavement. When he glanced toward the van, the license plate was facing the wrong direction as the guy sped off. "At least we know Jenny was alive a couple of hours ago. I'm terrified of what he'll do to her since she tried to escape."

Without a word, Dobbs nodded and started the engine. His jaw clenched, clueing Tara in on how worried he was about the girl. She turned, hiding her own fears, and stared out of the passenger window while he pulled out on to the street.

He drove west in the direction the man had headed when he left the station. The road ran parallel to the busy interstate carrying them to more boroughs farther away. Tara didn't want to think about him merging onto the interstate and driving to another state. Out of their jurisdiction. Out of their clutches.

She gripped the seatbelt strap tighter. Another innocent person was dead because of that monster still on the loose. It would be easy to blame herself, but she couldn't go there.

She had to stay focused, stay grounded and think about how they could catch the bastard, even if they had to work with other law enforcements in another state.

One thing made her feel a little better. They now had a little more information on the kidnapper and they knew what he was driving. They'd put out a BOLO on him and an Amber alert on Jenny. Hopefully someone would see something and call it in. According to Chief Haynes, leads had been pouring in all day. Over one hundred calls had been made stating they'd seen the girl at different locations, but none had panned out so far.

Knowing he was armed and even more dangerous than they'd realized sent a cold chill down her spine.

Tara had another thought. They had rescued his victims early this morning. Did that mean he was changing his method of kidnapping and holding several young girls, at once? Was he planning on kidnapping more to replace his harem? Or, was Jenny his only target now? That wouldn't make sense. One wouldn't satisfy him. Most perverts with his M.O. usually needed more and more girls as time went along to get their 'fix'. One wasn't enough and then two wasn't enough and so on. He may have kidnapped Jenny to get back at her, but he wouldn't be able to stop with just her.

She spoke into the silence. "He's going to kidnap some more girls. Possibly start tonight and continue over several days."

Dobbs glanced her way and nodded. "I believe he will, too. But, will he stick to his same routine and pick girls out of the five-mile radius of the others, or will he branch out since he knows we're on to him?"

Tara rubbed the back of her head. A lingering headache from the blow she'd taken earlier was getting worse by the minute. "He had a reason for picking that area. Maybe he lives close by or drives through the area every day to and from work. If he deviates, I don't think he'll go out much further. I say we start by having officers start patrolling that area, then move out when we need to."

Dobbs pulled to a stop in front of the police station. "If you want to do that, I'll check in to see if we got lucky enough and found fingerprints on the gas pump that are in the system." He smiled wryly. "I pity the lab techs. Can you imagine how many smeared fingerprints are probably on that one pump?"

Tara grinned and unhooked her seat belt. "Yes, but we only need the one."

* * *

Tara slumped at her desk, her cell phone to her ear, trying to assure Jake that she was all right. "I'm fine, Jake. Yes, I swear I'm fine. They wouldn't have released me from the emergency room if anything was wrong." She grinned into the phone. "No, I didn't threaten to handcuff them to the bed if they didn't release me. Will I see you tonight?" As the owner of an art gallery, Jake traveled the world looking for new pieces to display in his gallery.

"The art show wrapped up early. I'll fly home tonight. I plan to pamper you with a good meal, a little wine and a neck rub...plus more if you're up to it," he told her.

"It depends if I can get you up to it, which I'm sure I can, then I'll want the more."

"Naughty, naughty girl." His deep, soft and sexy voice sizzled across the line.

Sizzling all over herself, Tara laughed, delighted she would see her sexy man, soon. "See you tonight." She hung up and turned to see Dobbs standing in the doorway with a smirk on his face. It was obvious he'd overheard Jake's comment. "Don't say a word."

"Can't help it. You naughty girl. I didn't know you had that kinky side."

"You're just jealous of Jake, because you don't have a woman in your life. Don't you wish you could find someone as naughty as me?" she teased.

"Hell, yes. I won't lie. I do. But, it's kind of hard to find one when the only women I have time to see is laying in the morgue on a cold slab. I need to get out more." He sighed an 'Oh woe is me' sigh.

"Yes, I would say finding one alive who would put up with you would be harder, but I have faith in you, partner. You can do it."

"Bite me, Woods."

* * *

The new girl was pretty with her long, blonde hair and blue eyes the color of his favorite cola can, and she was smart, a straight A student. She could be an Olympian, a teacher, or even a lawyer when she grew up. Maybe even the President of the United States.

If, she were alive.

He smoothed her silky hair back from her face. Using two fingers he forced her eyelids closed, hiding her beautiful eyes forever. He leaned down to kiss her on the lips once more before he stood. Fastening his jeans, he laughed out loud and shivered in remembered ecstasy. Oh God, what a thrill. A thrill he could never do without. He already anticipated the next time. Yes siree.

He was born to kill.

CHAPTER SEVEN

Chief Haynes stuck his head into Tara's office. Tara and Dobbs looked up from their dinner from their favorite deli.

Chief Haynes frowned. "Sorry you two, but you'll have to eat on the run. Just got a call. They found another girl near the same area as the others."

Tara felt all of the blood drain from her face. Her hand went to her heart. She was scared to ask, but had to. "Jenny?"

"No. Sorry. I should have said that at the beginning. But, this looks to be the same M.O. as the others. Strangulation. Young girl around the same age as the others. Blonde hair and blue eyes. Coroner is headed to the scene now. I need you two down there, pronto."

"Yes Sir." Tara and Dobbs rose, dumped their half-eaten sandwiches into the trash and hurried to their car.

* * *

The scene was horrendous, but Tara blocked everything from her mind except the evidence before her. The young girl's body had been found in a small dried-up creek behind her house by a neighbor walking his dog. He'd called the police right away.

Twenty minutes later, the dog owner was still throwing up his guts. Tara felt like doing the same. The girl, a pre-teen, was lying on her back in a bed of dried blood. She was filleted open from the joining of her legs, up and through her chest bone to her neck. Her heart and liver were missing. This one was different from the other two recent victims who had only been raped and strangled.

Could there be two different serial killers in the same neighborhood? A copycat, maybe? Or, was the same one becoming more demented as he killed? Tara would put her money on the third choice.

The only similarities among the three murders were that all three girls were around the same age and all three wore a necklace of bruises around their necks. The other two had been raped before they were killed. Medical Examiner, Ben Marks would determine if this one had been molested, as well. He, as well as the forensic team, was already on the scene collecting evidence.

Tara stood outside the crime scene tape observing as much as she could without disturbing the evidence. She wanted to be in the middle of things, but knew they would kick her out if she tried. She finally turned away and walked over to where Dobbs was questioning the man who found the girl. A large Labrador was leashed beside him.

Dobbs looked up and saw her. "Mr. Sanders, this is Detective Woods. She'll be working this case with me. You were about to tell me why you were in the area."

Dan Sanders, a tall, strawberry-blond man in his early thirties, was still pale. He swallowed hard and shook Tara's hand. He stood with his back to the victim, blocking the crime from his sight, if not his memory. "Like I was saying, I jog this way every evening around four. I keep the same schedule on the weekend, but this evening, I was on a conference call at home and was running late by about two hours." He pointed behind him. "Mattie Wilson lived two houses down from me. God, I can't believe this. She was just a baby when her parents moved into the neighborhood. This is going to kill Mike and Joanie. Mattie is everything to them."

"Were you close to them, Mr. Sanders? Did you socialize with them?"

He nodded and wiped away a tear. "My wife, Karen and Joannie are best friends. Dan and I work together in a Tech firm downtown. We have a daughter just a year older than Mattie. So, yeah, we do a lot of barbecues and things like that. Oh, God. I just realized this could have easily been my daughter lying there." He broke down, sobbing into his hands.

Tara and Dobbs gave him a moment to grieve. Finally, the man wiped his tears away with his sleeve and looked up at them, the look in his eyes determined. "I want to be the one who breaks it to Mike and Joannie and my wife. They'll appreciate it more coming from someone they know and care about."

Tara looked over at Dobbs and then shook her head. "I'm sorry, but that would go against police procedure. We'll send someone out to talk to them, and we'd appreciate it if you wouldn't contact them until we do have a chance to let the family know what has happened."

Sanders glanced up in panicked confusion. He stammered. "But, I'll be seeing Mike this evening."

"We'll stop by their home as soon as we leave here and break the sad news to them. He should still be at home. And, we'll need you to stop by headquarters as soon as possible this morning. We'll need to get your DNA and then question all four of you and your daughter later this evening. It's only protocol. We're hoping you can give us some more information that might help us find this monster."

Losing his determined look, Sanders gave a short, defeated nod. Reaching into his back pocket he reached for his billfold and pulled out a business card. He handed the card with his phone number to Dobbs then cited off his home address. "I'll be in later."

Turning, he jogged back the way he'd come to do the painful task of telling his wife the horrific news. Knowing his friends would soon be getting the gut-wrenching knock on their door informing them their child had been brutally murdered was unthinkable.

Tara and Dobbs walked back to Bens' side. "Did it happen here or elsewhere and brought here after she was murdered?"

"Oh, no doubt it happened here. Too much blood for it to have been done anywhere else." Ben glanced back at the girl. "Poor thing. At least he killed her before he mutilated her. What a way to die." He looked at Dobbs. "It was late evening. A nice, family neighborhood. I can't believe no one heard her screams and reported it."

"Maybe they did and didn't want to get involved."

Tara rubbed the back of her neck and looked around the area. A community of nice, homes owned by blue-collared residents sat side by side on both sides of the road. "It's a working neighborhood. Most could still be at work or heading home. I'll have Jackson ask around to see if anyone was at home and heard something out of the ordinary."

* * *

Getting back in the car, Dobbs and Tara drove away from the scene to inform the parents their daughter was dead. This was the worst part of her job and she hated delivering the devastating news to the family. She got through the process by knowing her sympathy and kindness, in a way, comforted the grieving.

There was nothing more they could do for Mattie. But, there were plenty they could do for Jenny. Tara was already on the phone with Officer Jackson to get him started on the questioning in the neighborhood.

Dobbs' cell phone rang. Recognizing the number, he smiled. "Hi Mom."

"Hello, Son. Your Dad's here with me. How are you?"

"I'm doing good, Mom. Are you guys okay?" His parents had retired the year before and moved to Florida to a nice retirement village. They were thriving and quiet content in the golf and tennis world they lived in with their new friends.

"We're doing great. We wanted to call you to let you know we're flying in to New York tomorrow to visit you. Your dad and I miss you, Son. I know your apartment is cramped, so I've booked a hotel close by. We thought we could take you to lunch tomorrow and then dinner and a show later. How does that sound?"

Dobbs hesitated. He hated disappointing his parents and he would really love to spend some time with them but, they had never understood everything his job entailed or the multiple dangers involved. He didn't want them worried. They thought he sat behind a desk all day. Just a little white lie to ease their minds. "Mom. This is really a bad time. Tara and I are working on a case. We'll be working long hours, non-stop until it's solved."

"Nonsense. I know your job is important, but you have to eat. You can stop long enough to eat lunch and visit with your parents for a while. We haven't seen you in ages, and we know you don't take care of yourself. I worry. I'm a mother. That's what we do. Worry."

"Mom. I really can't. I would love to, though."

"Son. We'll see you for lunch tomorrow at noon at Pierre's. No argument. And bring Tara along. I like that girl and we haven't seen her in ages, either. You need to settle down and find you a good woman who will take care of you. Then I can stop worrying."

Dobbs groaned and slid a glance over at Tara. She'd gotten off the phone and was listening in on his conversation in delight, with a full blown grin. No, it was a full-blown smirk. "Mom. I know what you're doing and it won't work. So, stop your matchmaking. Please."

His mom chuckled. "See you and Tara tomorrow, Son, and give her my love." She hung up.

Which was a good thing, because his Mom had never heard him cuss, and she would've gotten an earful if she's stayed on the line.

CHAPTER EIGHT

Jenny lay in a fetal position for what seemed like hours and hours, but even with the tinted windows in the SUV, she could tell it was still daylight, maybe early evening.

Her kidnapper had stopped the vehicle moments before and left her. She was finally alone and could take the chance of making a little noise inside the van.

Frantically, Jenny began working hard on her restraints knowing he would be back at any time. Sweat ran down her face and her raw, bloody wrists burned with every twist, but she continued working them back in forth inside the chains. She might have this one and only chance. Her abductor was growing more unpredictable and dangerous.

He'd ranted and cursed her for trying to escape, blaming her for making him kill the guy. But, until now he'd remained behind the wheel driving for miles and miles down side roads, going from borough to borough and going to God knows where. One moment, he would be screaming, cussing and pounding the steering wheel. The next, he was laughing at how he'd gotten away. Now, all was quiet and she fought her chains.

Suddenly, without warning the back door swung up. She screamed as he reached in, jerked her out and dragged her to a large, metal building. It looked creepily abandoned. Like ghost abandoned. She shivered.

TANGLE WITH TARA

He threw her inside and followed behind. Cobwebs clung to her face, hair and clothing. She screeched and shuddered with no way of brushing off the webs.

Grabbing the tight chain around her painful wrists, he slapped her hard across her cheek and threw her to the hard, concrete floor. She skidded across the hard surface and felt the skin peel away from her arm.

Whimpering with tears streaking down her face, she looked up defiantly at her assailant, trying to be strong. "Why are you doing this? Let me go."

He just grinned down at her for a moment with a look in his eyes she'd never seen before. Intuitively, she knew what it was. Lust. Pure lust. Fear gripped her soul and she scooted further away.

He turned and walked back out the door. She let out a shuddering sigh of relief. But, her relief was short lived. Before she could get to her feet and try to run, he was back. This time he held a heavy chain in his hand. Grabbing her hands, he looped the chain around them and dragged the other end to a nearby two by four used as a brace. Pulling a lock from his pocket, he hooked it through the chain links. When the lock clicked back in place, she felt doomed.

Defeated for the moment, she scooted out of the way of his fists and leaned against the filthy wall behind her.

The monster started for the door. Terrified he would leave her here to die, she rallied and struggled with the chains. She screamed out. "You can't leave me here."

His evil grin appeared. "You won't be here long." He turned and walked out the door. Moments later, she heard the SUV's motor rev up and he drove off.

Sobbing, she slid to the floor with her knees drawn up to her chest. He'd lied to her. She would never leave. No one would ever find her here. She hadn't seen any other buildings or humans around when he forced her inside. Hysteria built. They would only find her bones, days, months, or even years later.

* * *

A family member or a close friend of a murdered victim usually became the cop's first suspects.

As the usual procedure, she and Dobbs questioned both the grieving parents of Mattie Wilson and the Sanders family, the man who found the girl.

Eventually, they eliminated both families from murdering the girl. They all had reliable alibis.

Tara knew it was a waste of time, anyway. No one close to Wilson family had anything to do with the disappearance of any of the murdered girls.

They were dealing with a crazed serial killer, and the latest girl, Mattie Wilson, was at least his third victim they knew anything about. Tara was anxious to hear the medical examiner's report after the autopsy.

* * *

Tara had never known Ben' instincts to be wrong, she thought as she walked into his domain. This was another part of her job she dreaded. She hated everything about the morgue, the particular, pungent smell of the body and the chemicals, the coldness penetrating the room and the visual sight of the victim cut open on the table. As their usual procedure, Ben handed her a scented cloth to hold over her face.

"What did you find?" Tara motioned to the girl.

Ben sighed and removed his gloves. "Other than the obvious wounds and the strangulation, there's a visible bruising inside her thighs, and bruises on her arms and back. The girl fought a hard fight before the assault. Since there is bruising already, I put her time of death around three or four hours ago."

"What about DNA? Skin under the nails, semen. Please, give me something to go on."

"No semen found, but there was penetration. No scrapes of skin or loose hair on her, though. Sorry. I did find particles of clothing beneath her nails. I sent it to the lab for testing."

"Guess that's better than nothing. Maybe we'll luck out on the material. Thanks Ben." Dammit, for once couldn't this creep screw up?

Tara looked down at the girl. From her parent's statement earlier, the girl had been a sweet innocent girl when she got out of bed this morning. Everything could change in a mere second.

CHAPTER NINE

Albert Jones wasted no time in securing another S.U.V. for his purpose. He was getting pretty damn good at stealing vehicles in broad daylight. How people could be so stupid in this day and time to leave their keys in their cars while they made a quick trip into a store still befuddled him. Didn't these people watch the news? Car theft was at its all-time highest in a decade. Jeeze. Some people deserved to be robbed.

He drove out of the convenience store parking lot in a newer model white Chevrolet Equinox and headed straight into the heavy traffic, blending in with all the other white vehicles on the highway. Reaching for his cell phone he punched in the numbers to call his wife. He hated lying to his sweet Mary, but she would never question him when he told her he was working a double shift. He'd used the excuse often. It would be his son who'd be so disappointed his dad couldn't be at the game this evening.

It couldn't be helped. It was that girl's fault. No. It was that woman detective's fault. If she hadn't broken up his little party, he'd be home with his family getting ready to go to Timmy's game.

TANGLE WITH TARA

All her fault.

His fist hit the steering wheel hard, jerking him into the next lane, almost side-swiping another car. He forced himself to calm down. The last thing he needed was to draw attention to himself. He'd make her pay if it was the last thing he ever did. An ugly grin appeared on his face and he almost felt giddy. He couldn't wait until she met his latest trophy.

* * *

Around nine o'clock Tuesday evening, Tara ended her call with Jake with a loud sigh. She stared down at her desk. Their date night was postponed. Again. Jake was a saint and Tara knew he truly understood her choice of a career and her need to find Jenny, but even he had his limits. His short, abrupt replies before they ended the conversation told her as much.

She cursed and ran her fingers through her hair in frustration, before resting her forehead on the desk. "I'm going to end up an old maid or maybe a cat lady with fifty cats and a vibrator to keep me company in my old age."

"Now, I had another scenario in mind."

Tara screeched and rolled backwards. Her chair hit the wall behind her and she bounced forward. Coming to a sudden stop, her hardened gaze rested on the man leaning against her door frame laughing.

Dobbs grinned and continued. "I was thinking more of you, at the ripe old age of eighty, pole dancing in the retirement home with dirty old men asking for a lap dance. You could still have the vibrator if you want."

"Dammit, Dobbs. If you ever want to have children, you will never sneak up on me like that, again," she growled, foot-rolling herself back to her desk.

He shrugged and strolled further into her office, taking a chair across from her desk. "I didn't want to interrupt your conversation with yourself. It was getting interesting."

Her eyes narrowed. "Let it go, Dobbs."

He grinned and wagged his finger in front of her face. "Oh, no...no, my friend. I will store this tidbit of information in my memory bank and pull it out when I need a little blackmail leverage."

A smile formed and Tara leaned back in her chair and crossed her arms. "It's going to be so lovely visiting with your parents. I have so much to tell your sweet mama about her son's love life, or shall I say lack of. I bet she can find you a date if I tell her how desperate you are to find a woman. Maybe she'll call her best friend's worn out, middle-aged daughter who happens to be looking for a father for her ten children or something."

Dobbs grin disappeared. "You wouldn't dare. You know how my mama is."

"Oh, but I would, and you know it."

Dobbs brows drew together. He opened his mouth to respond, but stopped when Tara's cell phone rang.

"Detective Woods." Tara listened for a moment and then ended the call. She looked up at Dobbs, her shoulders sagged. "That was Missing Persons. Another girl from Jenny's and Stacy's neighborhood has come up missing. He's branching out, possibly widening his playing field."

Dobbs nodded, with a thoughtful look as he stared into her eyes. "Either that or he's moving his playing field closer to you."

* * *

Fifteen minutes later, Tara and Dobbs arrived at the missing girl's apartment that was just two blocks from Stacy's and Jenny's home and her own apartment. The front door stood wide open. Missing Person's Detective Lisa Gunter was inside, interviewing the parents. The Forensic team was busy taking DNA samples, prints and photographs of the scene.

With an okay from the lead crime scene investigator and checking in with the first responder, Tara and Dobbs walked through the foyer and into the spacious living area to greet the detective and the missing girl's parents.

The apartment's simple, but clean decor as well as the parent's clothing shouted middle-class. At first glance, Tara could tell it was a loving home with the many photographs of the family, especially the missing daughter and a younger son, placed throughout the room.

Detective Gunter glanced up and nodded. "Detectives. I figured you two would show up for this one, since it's closely related to your own case. I was just getting started, if you want to sit in."

"We do. Thank you."

"Great. Mr. and Mrs. Talken, this is Detective Woods and Detective Dobbs. They may have some questions for you, as well."

Tara nodded to the thirty-something couple. Worry, deeply etched on the father's face, turned to concern as he glanced down at his wife. He rocked her back and forth while she cried into a tissue.

"We'll answer any questions you have. Just please bring our baby back to us."

Detective Hunter nodded. "I promise you, we'll do everything in our power to bring Candace home. First Mrs. Talken, do you have a recent picture of your daughter that we can have?"

The mother dabbed her eyes and nodded. "She has several selfies on her phone I can send you. We found her phone on the doorstep this morning. She never goes anywhere without that phone. I'm so worried." She leaned against her husband's shoulder as fresh tears ran down her cheeks. Her husband squeezed her shoulders a moment until she calmed. He handed her a fresh Kleenex. She straightened, her eyes red and swollen. "I also have her latest school picture on the mantle. I'll get them for you." She rose. Weariness slowed her steps.

"Thank you. That will be a big help. Now, Mr. Talken when was the last time you and your wife saw your daughter?"

"Last night around ten o'clock when she went to bed. She left around six this morning to babysit for a couple a few blocks down the road. We were still asleep. When she didn't show up this evening, I called the couple and the mother said she'd dropped her off at one this afternoon. She said she'd waited until Candace got to the front door before driving off. My wife and I were both gone at the time."

"What about her friends? Could she have gone to see one of them?" Tara asked.

"We called all of her friends and they haven't seen her."

Detective Hunter looked up from her notes. "A boyfriend?"

"I don't think she has one now. She'd broken up with this young boy about a month ago. I didn't have much use for him. There was something about him that hit the father panic button in me even though he came from a good family."

"Was she seeing anyone else that you knew about?" Tara knew the teen girls these days didn't always tell their parents everything happening in their lives.

Mr. Talken shook his head. "As far as I know she wasn't seeing anyone else. Of course, at fifteen, I've only allowed her to go on group dates or go to a well-chaperoned party at people's homes that we know. She knows I wouldn't allow her to be alone with a guy. I don't think she would ever sneak off to be with a boy. Or, maybe that's the father in me talking. I would hope she wouldn't, anyway."

Mrs. Talken walked back into the room with her daughter's phone and an eight by ten photograph. She handed both over to Detective Hunter.

"Thank you. May I keep the phone for a while? And, her computer if she has one. We'll need to check all of her calls, messages and her social media sites to see if it will give us a lead."

"Yes, of course." She left the room again and returned shortly with her daughter's laptop. "I know we're overly protective, but we only allow her to use a password that we provided for her. She's a good girl, but there are a lot of predators out there, so we keep an eye on who she's talking to on those sites. Here's the password." She handed a post-it-note to the Detective. She sank back down beside her husband.

"Speaking of predators, have either of you seen anyone unfamiliar or suspicious acting hanging around in the neighborhood lately? Or, the neighbors? Have they mentioned anything unusual" Dobbs asked.

Mr. Talken thought for a moment and shook his head. "None that I can think of but, I'm at work most of the day. Honey, have you seen anyone?"

"No. We've lived here long enough to know everyone on this street and a few over from us. I recognized Detective Woods immediately. I've seen her jogging by the house most mornings. And, the man a few blocks over walks his dog at the same time every day and has for years. Our neighbor down the street came by pushing a stroller. Just the usual people I see every day."

Detective Hunter pulled a card out and handed it to the husband. "Thank you very much. I think that's all I need for now. We'll do everything we can to find Candace and bring her home safe. If either of you think of anything else or hear from your daughter, give me a call immediately. I'll be in touch."

Tara, Dobbs and Hunter left the home. Standing beside their cars, they studied the picture of Candace. She and Jenny didn't look a lot alike, but there was an eerie resemblance with their size, age, and blonde hair. Enough to put Tara on edge. She nodded toward Hunter. "Thanks Lisa. We owe you one for calling us in on this case."

"No problem. Usually, I'd want the girl missing longer than a few hours before starting an investigating, but this sounded too similar to the case you guys are working. Do you think it's the same guy?"

Tara met her eyes. "Unfortunately, I do."

CHAPTER TEN

Jenny knew she'd never free herself from the heavy chains, but, she was smart. Her parents and teachers told her so. She would outsmart and outthink her captor. He didn't seem too bright. Who in their right mind would shoot an elderly man in broad daylight with witnesses all around? No one. He was stupid. Stupid. Stupid.

She wiped the tears from her cheeks and forced herself to think, but only felt guilty. Her mom would ground her for a month for calling anyone stupid. But, she'd ground her for another month if she didn't fight for her life.

She would fight with everything she had. She would be strong and survive for her mom. She couldn't leave her mom alone like her dad had. Her mom needed her.

She tried to think things through. Deep in her heart, she knew her friend Tara and her sexy looking partner, Detective Dobbs were hunting for her right now. Tara would never let anyone hurt her, but, she had to use her wits until Tara and Dobbs found her. But, oh God, it was so hard to think!

Determined, she glanced around the building, looking for any means of escape. There were two roll-up doors on the far end that she could see. They reminded her of the garage doors at home , only a lot larger.

Inside the metal building looked as if it had been abandoned and empty for a long time. It was dirty, cold, and spooky. She could see stars twinkling in the sky through the only small window high on one wall. Even if she could free herself of the chains, there was no way she could reach the window to climb out. There was nothing to push beneath it to climb up on, or any other door that she could see.

Jenny glanced back toward the metal garage doors. They were her only means of escape. When he returned she knew what she had to do. Getting him to remove her chains and leaving them off would be tricky, but she had to think of some way to talk him into it. She had to.

Her heart dropped. What if he locked the garage doors from the outside when he left? What would she do then? Tears threatened, and the thought of escape seemed hopeless, but she straightened her shoulders. Her mom would tell her to think smart. And, Tara would want her to fight for her life. The thought of them finding her lifeless body spurred her on. "That....that, sorry Mom for saying the bad word, but that bastard will not win. I will fight him until you find me." The sound of her voice sounding so strong in the silence gave her more courage.

Jenny cocked her head to the side and her breath caught. Was that the sound of gravel crunching and a loud purr of a motor coming close to the building? Then, the motor shut off right outside. She scooted back against the cold wall and trembled. He was back.

She heard a scratching sound, then one door moved upward. He appeared in the doorway, wearing that terrible sinister smile as he looked at her. Then, suddenly he disappeared.

Oh God. She couldn't see him. What was he doing? She freaked out, trying to see outside the doors. Where did he go?

Moments later, he reappeared with a large bundle thrown over his shoulder. He dropped it next to her, and it was only when she felt a tug on her chain did she realize the bundle was another girl who was being chained beside her.

* * *

Around ten o'clock Tuesday evening, Tara's feet ached like the dickens. She'd been on them for hours. Removing her running shoes, she massaged one burning foot and sighed in relief. She leaned her head back against her desk chair and gave her other foot the same soothing treatment.

Dobbs sat in the chair across from her with his feet propped up on her desk. He yawned and wiggled into a comfortable position.

Officer Jackson leaned against the wall and stared out of Tara's office window. Running his fingers through his gray hair, he glanced at Tara and Dobbs and muttered a curse. "It's been one helluva day."

"Yes, it has. Unfortunately, it's not over for us." Booting up his tablet sitting on his lap, Dobbs began scrolling through the notes he'd made on the latest girl's murder. "I want to read everything, again. Even though it seems like for the thousandth time. We're missing something."

Tara emitted a weary sigh and waved toward the chair next to Dobbs. "Jackson, might as well take a load off while I wash up. The pizza I ordered earlier is on its way. We can eat a bite while we go over these notes. Then, you can go on home."

Jackson nodded. "Sounds good. I'm starving." After Tara left the room, he started to sit when a knock on the door sounded. Reaching the door first, he paid the delivery guy for the pizza. Placing the box on the desk, he reached for a slice of pizza before sitting. He picked off a piece of pepperoni and stuck it in his mouth.

Tara returned to her desk and grabbed a napkin to lay her pizza on. She bit into her slice and chewed. She was almost too tired to eat. It'd been almost sixteen hours since she'd received the frightening call about Jenny's disappearance. She needed to be concentrating on the latest murder and let the Missing Persons search for Jenny and Candace, but the girls' immediate danger took over her thoughts.

They'd found the abandoned van they were hunting. The owner of the convenience store reported it to the police while they were investigating another stolen vehicle from the same store. The surveillance video confirmed it was their man who'd left the vehicle and stolen the latest S.U.V. . So far, they hadn't found any prints. But, the drops of blood found in the back of the van matched Jenny's blood type. Anger and fear killed her appetite. She swallowed hard.

He had hurt her.

She'd bled.

Only a few drops, but she'd bled. If it was the last thing she ever did, Tara would help put the bastard away for the rest of his sorry life.

Officer Jackson interrupted her troubled thoughts. He leaned forward and reached for another slice. He pointed the triangle wedge toward Tara and Dobbs. "What has me puzzled is why he keeps certain girls and kills the others. How is he deciding who he holds hostage and who he mutilates? I don't believe either is a random act. He knows his prey beforehand. I mean, the young girl they found this morning. She wasn't missing long enough for her to be one of his kidnapped victims. What was it about her that made him decide to kill her and not keep?"

Dobbs looked up from his tablet and wiped the pizza sauce from his chin with his napkin. He shrugged. "Who knows how evil, twisted minds work? It could be their hair color, physical build, their smile, maybe. Whatever it is triggers different emotions in different people. Usually, they associate something in the girls similar to whomever hurt them in the past or to someone they look up to and loved, but who left or hurt them."

Tara took a drink from her soda. "We know he likes blondes. Jenny, Candace and Mattie are all blondes. The six girls we rescued were blondes or had light brown hair. None were the same height or build. Different eye colors. All around the same age. All from the same area, going to the same school. Not all in the same grade, though. But, they knew each other from seeing the others around school. I'll bet you money they'll also know Jenny, Candace and Mattie."

Dobbs nodded. "That's easy to check out. So, who hurt him? His mother? Sister? Or, a girlfriend, maybe? A female, definitely."

Tara ran the choices through her mind. "It could be any or all. I say we talk to Cindy Tablor. Get her to analyze and give us a background on what we know so far. If she's still in her office this late."

Tara picked up the phone and made a call to the second floor where Cindy, their criminal profiler's office was located. When she answered, Tara put them on speaker phone and greeted her friend with, "I'm glad I caught you before you left. We need your help. The case we're working on is time-sensitive."

She gave a tired laugh. "You do know what time it is, right? You almost missed me. I was walking out the door. What can I help you with? I know you wouldn't have called this late unless you needed me."

"Believe me. I do." Tara filled her in on the case.

Cindy listened closely to everything Tara told her before responding. "I'll need to work on this some more with more information, but my guess is that he was hurt at a young age. We know from the description given to you by the woman whose husband he shot that the perp is a white male around forty years old, so, you might want to check all child abuse cases around...say...1975 or '76 when he was born thru the next twenty years or so. Just listening to you in general, I don't think he would've left or moved far from his childhood home. He has close connections here. The one who hurt him would keep him close. Their talons would bind them and not let him go."

"If the person is still alive." Dobbs said.

"True. If it were me, I'd start in the five mile radius you spoke about. If nothing is found, you can span out to the other boroughs. I think you'll find him close, because I agree with you. I think he has a grudge against Tara for messing with his cravings. And, that's what he has. He craves the excitement of the actual kidnapping and sexual assaults. He can't give all of that up. Plus, it sounds like he wants a pissing match with Tara."

Tara sighed. "I was afraid you would say that. Jackson, can you stay with us a little longer and check this out for us?"

"Don't you worry about me. I'll get started on it right away. Otherwise I'd sit at home wide awake, wondering what I could do to help." Jackson rose and left the office waving away Tara's thanks.

Tara turned to Dobbs while she spoke to Cindy. "Is it possible that we're totally off on this? He may have just been born a bad egg with a perfect upbringing and lucky enough to dodge the system."

"From my experience, that's probably not the case."

Tara sighed. "Thank you, Cindy. You've been a big help."

"My pleasure. Goodnight. Let me know if I can help in anyway."

After they ended the call, Dobbs shrugged, his eyes cold. "We're not quitting until we get Jenny and Candace back and stop that bastard."

Tara's chin dropped to her chest so he couldn't see the deep emotions she was feeling. Combined utter weariness and gratitude for her partner and her team's willingness to keep on almost brought her to tears. "Thank you."

Not wanting Dobbs' worry or sympathy, she needed to get a hold of her emotions and act like nothing was wrong. She glanced up and grinned. "Let's go whip some butt."

Her cell phone rang before she could stand. Glancing at the phone number, she quickly answered. "Stacy? Have you heard anything from Jenny?"

"No. Nothing. I don't want to bother you but, I couldn't just sit around doing nothing. I wanted to let you know I contacted the Talkens earlier when I heard their daughter was missing, same as Jenny. We've started a neighborhood watch. We're also going door to door showing Jenny's and Candace's pictures. Some of Jenny's and Candace's friends are posting their pictures up and down the streets and store windows where they can. This is okay, isn't it?"

"Stacy, I'd rather you let our officers do the questioning. They are trained in this. Everything you're trying to do is wonderful. We can use the extra help. But, this guy is very dangerous. You could be putting yourself in danger if you happen to knock on the right door. We don't know who he is or where he lives." Tara told her, trying not to lecture her friend. She didn't need Stacy and the other's in harm's way.

"I understand. But, that's my daughter. I need to do something." Tears choked her up. "We weren't having any luck, anyway. We thought they might open up more to the parents than they would police officers, but we learned nada. No one knows anything about the girls. They told us they would keep a watchful eye out, though.

"Stacy, you've been a big help. And, I'm glad you're keeping busy. But, try to get some rest, too. Okay? I want you to know we're doing everything possible on this end."

"I know you are and I am so proud I have you searching for Jenny. Don't worry about me. I'm in for the night and will try to rest and start fresh in the morning. Goodnight."

TANGLE WITH TARA

Tara hit the 'end' button. She didn't know how in the hell Stacy could be proud she was on the job. When, she should hate her for putting her daughter in danger. Her shock would wear off sooner or later and the hate would come. Tara dreaded the moment.

CHAPTER ELEVEN

When Albert Jones drove up the short, paved driveway to his home, he was two hours late. Killing the motor, he rested his forehead against the steering wheel, trying to calm his hectic thoughts and rapid heart rate.

He could do this.

He'd lied to his wife and son so many times over the past years, and they always believed him. They didn't need to know he'd pulled a short shift at work today, instead of the overtime his wife would think. He should be an actor. The thought brought a huge grin to his face. He *was* an actor!

He could do this.

Raising his head, he wiped his sweaty palms against his pants legs and took a deep breath. Show time. Grabbing his keys from the ignition, he opened the door and stepped out before his wife came out to check on him, or ask him about the different van he was driving.

Walking up the sidewalk , he took a moment to admire the older suburban home he'd provided for him and his family. It wasn't much, and it wasn't new. Just a two-bedroom frame that needing a fresh coat of paint, but he'd worked hard giving his family a roof over their heads, and, it was home.

Most of the time he didn't earn the money the way his wife thought he did, but he still worked enough at his dead end job to keep his boss happy. He brought home enough money a week to take care of his family. Legal or illegal. Didn't matter to him. He earned it and was proud of what they owned. Straightening his shoulders and standing taller, he opened the door and entered.

His life returned to normal.

Albert took a moment to relish the familiar sounds of his wife, Mary, cooking dinner in the kitchen. Mouth-watering aromas drifted out into the foyer where he stood. His nostrils flared and his stomach rumbled from hunger. It had been hours since he'd eaten and he'd worked up a huge appetite. He hated it when he had to miss meals. Food served on china was precious to him, something he would never willingly do without, again.

Walking down the short hallway toward the kitchen, he heard the T.V. playing in the living room. He glanced through the open doorway. Timmy was sprawled out on the couch watching his favorite sports channel. Baseball. Oh yes, the sights and smells of normality.

"Hey, you two. I'm home." He walked into the updated kitchen with all new appliances and gave his wife a kiss on the cheek. His wife deserved the new stove and refrigerator he'd bought her the month before for her birthday. "Hi, Hon. Sorry I'm late. Boss asked me to work over again this evening. Something smells wonderful. I'm starving."

Mary smiled and turned back to the stove. "Dinner's almost ready. Wash up and get Tim. I'll put the food on the table. Then, you can tell us about your long day at work."

When he returned to the table with his son in tow, he sat down and waited for his family to join him. Platters of delicious smelling food filled the table.

After Albert led the prayer, his wife dished up their plates and they began to chat about their day. Timmy took the lead, going on non-stop about the baseball game Albert had missed that evening.

"I hate it when you aren't there to coach my games, Dad. Old man Jenson isn't as good as you. He almost lost us our game today. He wouldn't let Marty bat when it was his turn because Marty plowed into the other team's second baseman and made him twist his ankle. He didn't do it on purpose." Timmy reached for a roll.

"I'm sure he didn't son. I'm sorry I couldn't make the game. But, I promise, I'll try my best to be at your next game."

Timmy's shoulders sagged. "That's what you said last time."

"I'll try." Albert took the refilled plate from his wife and thanked her. He really tried to be a good father and husband. He wanted to be everything his own parents weren't able to give him while he was growing up. It was hard.

He forced away the unwanted memories of his father's early death from alcohol poisoning when Albert was only ten. And, of his mother's abusive addiction to heroin. The thoughts of his mother feeding him slop in a dog bowl while she kept him chained out in the shed was the worst. She was high. Always high. The many drunk 'husbands' she had over the years after his father's death would eat steak off of her fancy dinnerware his father had bought her. She would throw him the meat bone. She called it a treat and told Albert he should be thankful. The men would only laugh and carry her off to bed.

Captive in the basement with little learning, he was fourteen, the same age of his son now, before he ever ate on a plate or sat at a dinner table, or, felt a kind hand or heard a soft, drug-free voice.

His wife and son would never know her mother-in-law and his grandmother was buried deep beneath the basement's flooring only a few feet from where they sat enjoying dinner in what was once his parents' home.

The cops had believed his story that his mother abandoned him by running away with one of the many good-for-nothing men in her life. After taking one uneasy look at his battered and malnourished body, the contents of the basement with the chains and the dog bowls the men in uniform and the child services thought he was better off without his mom. They didn't waste much time looking for her.

Albert hid a grin from his son and wife. His mother was missing, alright. She made the grave mistake of forgetting to lock his chains after a night of partying. A mistake she would never make again.

Luckily, the foster life he'd led until he grew of age was much better than his life with his slut of a mother. He'd survived. But, he'd never forgotten.

He set his unwanted thoughts to the side. "This tastes wonderful, Hon."

His wife smiled and folded her napkin in her lap. "Thank you. I found this in the freezer. I guess I'd forgotten those packages were in there. I know how much you love liver and the heart so I laid it out to defrost this morning. It smells almost as good as fresh. Eat up, you two. Then, we'll have some berry cobbler with a big scoop of ice cream."

Albert looked at his son and grinned. "Yum. Our favorite."

"Oh, I forgot to tell you about my interesting news. The local cops stopped by and asked if we'd seen anything suspicious. They said a couple of teenage girls are missing and they found one dead not too far from us. They were stopping all over the neighborhood asking them the same question. I feel so horrible for those girls and their families." Mary told him.

Albert dropped his fork. It clattered onto his plate.

CHAPTER TWELVE

11:00 p.m., Tara hit the 'call end' button on her cell phone. Stacy said she was too restless, her nerves too edgy to sleep. The house was too quiet without Jenny. Tara spent the last ten minutes updating and comforting Stacy on what they knew so far. Which wasn't much.

Stacy's renewed sobs lashed at Tara's torn heart strings. All she could do at this time was to keep Stacy updated and assure her friend they were doing everything in their power to find Jenny. Tara wished she could've offered her more. Stacy deserved more.

Dobbs had gone back to his own office to work and maybe catch a short nap.

Tara sighed and rolled the growing tension from her aching shoulder blades trying to find comfort. Exhausted, she leaned her head against her chair and closed her heavy eyes. She must have dozed off, because her chin hitting her chest jerked her awake. She rubbed her eyes and yawned. Standing up, she stretched and rounded her desk. Caffeine. She needed caffeine. A strong cup of black coffee might wake her up. Her day was a long time away from ending. She couldn't stop now.

Minutes later, Tara struggled to reign in the temptation to kick the large silver and black coffee vending machine in the break room. Second thought, she kicked the coffee machine anyway and growled as a sharp pain ran up her foot. Her brows narrowed and her blood boiled. The blasted contraption took her money, the only change she had on her, and left her staring down into a cup of water with only a hint of murky coffee.

"Dammit." She chunked the cup into the trashcan. What happened to having a huge coffee pot in the precinct with the coffee strong, black as night and hours old? Who decided to change things around here? They should be tarred and feathered.

Knowing her nerves were on edge and the machine was in grave danger, she knew she needed to get out of the building for a while, clear her head, and wake up.

Walking next door, she peeked into Dobbs' office. His head was lying on his arms resting on the top of his desk. From his deep breathing and light snores, she knew he was sound asleep. Like her, he needed a break. Deciding to let him rest, she turned and walked down the hallway, past the busy officers on duty, some guiding their prisoners down the hallway to the booking room. With a wave to the night crew, she stepped out into the warm night air.

Noticing the full moon in the sky, she groaned and shook her head. The nutcases would be out tonight, keeping the night-shift on their toes. Tara patted the Glock .380 pistol inside her jacket, turned and began walking north, the moon and the street lights showing her way. A couple of blocks down was her favorite coffee shop, that thankfully was open twenty-four hours a day. The walk and the coffee would wake her up and give her an extra energy boost to keep working a few more hours. She might even take Dobbs a cup of coffee and a couple of donuts. Might.

A young couple strolled past, arm-in-arm. Tara smiled and thought of Jake, wishing they were able to find the time for a date and to be as carefree as the laughing couple snuggling against each other, not a care in the world. It had been ages since she and Jake had gone to a movie and dinner, or anything else for that matter. She missed him.

Remembering that her twenty-ninth birthday was coming up in another month, drove home the fact that her biological clock was quickly ticking away. Did she want kids? Sure, she wanted kids. But, she also wanted a career as a homicide detective. And, so far, she hadn't figured out how to have both. Or, how to keep her future children and future husband safe with the dangerous line of work she was in.

Or, to forget her childhood memories.

Her father, a New York City police officer, had been so careful to watch his back, but, he'd still fallen victim to a strung-out drug addict who'd killed him and Tara's mom leaving his eight-year-old daughter parentless. Seeing her parents lying in pools of blood would haunt her for the rest of her life.

Tara didn't know if she could or would ever take the chance of putting a child of hers through what she had, growing up without parents. She'd been lucky to have a loving aunt and uncle to take her in and raise her as their own. With her and Jake being the only child in each family, any kids they might have would have no one if something happened. They would fall into the hands of child welfare.

Tara knew firsthand from her line of work, the horrors some children faced when placed into unsatisfactory and unloving or abusive homes. They runaway and steal for food and clothes or god forbid, become victims of prostitution and white slavery.

She shuddered. Could she ever entertain the thought of having a child who might have to go through that kind of hell?

As a Homicide Detective who'd helped put murdering felons behind bars, she had several enemies, ones who threatened to get back at her for her part in putting them away for the rest of their lives. She couldn't fool herself into believing she was safe. Her parents were murdered. The same could happen to her and her future child. And, Jake. Would he be willing to take the chance? Or, in good conscience, could she even ask him to continue to be a part of her dangerous life? Could she not?

Tara shook off the dismal thoughts that played in the forefront of her mind. She'd deal with her worries later. She didn't have the luxury of thinking about her problems when Jenny was missing. "Keep your thoughts on the case, Tara girl. Your future is on hold until you find Jenny," she mumbled to herself.

The coffee shop was close enough for the sweet aroma of the pastries and the strong coffee blended to penetrate her nostrils. She walked faster, anticipating the treats.

And, then she heard a sound behind her. Footsteps.

CHAPTER THIRTEEN

As automatic as breathing, Tara's fingers gripped her holstered pistol as she spun around, hoping to see the young couple returning. Instead, a tall man stood behind her, dressed in all black clothing with a dark motorcycle mask covering his face. He held a short-barreled pistol pointed straight at her heart. Only his hard, glacial eyes were visible behind the woven cotton disguise.

"Pull out your gun nice and slow, then put it on the ground and slide it my way, detective." His calm, menacing voice never wavered. Neither did his hand as he pulled back the hammer with a soft click.

Tara took a split second to evaluate the situation. All he had to do was pull the trigger and he would hit his mark before she could move. He was bigger, taller and stronger than she was, and he'd gained the upper hand. But, she would bet her much needed coffee that he wouldn't have her extensive training in combat. She hoped.

Her only hope.

One thing deeply concerned her, though. He knew her. "You don't want to do this. You'll have cops crawling all over you within seconds." She kept eye contact. His eyes, she noticed were as blue and as cold as the bright neon sign hanging above the coffee shop's door. They also matched the blue lights on a police car she planned on shoving him into before the night was over.

"I'll take my chances." He waved his gun. "Do it, now."

Tara hesitated, and tried once more to reason with a madman. "Why are you doing this? If you wanted to rob me or kill me for a wrong you think I've done to you or your family, you would've done it as soon as I turned around. You still have time to walk away. I'm giving you that chance."

His grin turned pure evil. "I'm not going anywhere, Detective. I figured you might want to see your little friend, Jenny before I killed you both. One at a time. Not that you deserve the chance to say goodbye to her after destroying my entertainment. I think I'll hang on to my latest toy, though. I plan on having fun playing with her. "

A fighter's fury blasted through her veins. Her fingers clenched around her gun. "Where are they?"

"Patience. You'll find out soon enough. Your gun, Detective."

Tara slowly withdraw her service weapon, her mind flashing through possibilities. If she let him take her to Jenny and Candice, there was a small chance she could get herself and the two girls away from him. A bigger chance that he would kill all three of them before they could be rescued or get away.

Suddenly, her hand stilled and her heart rate increased. No. No. Not now. A tinkling of laughter behind him alerted her. The young couple was coming back, drawing closer with each step, unaware of the danger.

The masked man saw the couple. He shoved his gun into his jacket, and with one last warning look, he bolted forward, knocking her backwards onto the sidewalk, and bolted into the darkness.

Tara landed hard on her backside in a rush. She felt the pain streak up her back. The young couple raced toward her.

"Ma'am, are you okay?" One got on each side of her and helped her to her feet.

"I'm fine. Thank you." Ignoring the pain, she sprinted past the couple, raising her gun and yelling for the stranger to stop. He disappeared around the next corner. She'd lost precious seconds.

She grabbed her cell phone out of her back pocket and speed dialed Dobbs while she ran. When he answered, she screamed out in between sucking in air. "Man! Running. Attacked me. Has Jenny. He's heading toward 3rd and 22nd. Hurry."

"On my way. Don't do anything crazy, Tara," Dobbs said.

Tara's shoes slapped on the cobblestone pavement as she ran. She kept her eyes on the suspect and the surroundings. A block away, her perp dodged and pushed his way through and around the late shoppers and tourists heading home or their hotel room or out for an evening out on the town. Store owners were busy turning their Open signs around as they prepared to close for the night.

Up ahead, a construction crew working overtime tearing up one whole block of sidewalk was putting away their tools. Orange netting and cones enclosed the destruction site for safety. Concrete trucks and white pickup trucks with the construction logo on the side of doors lined the sides of the street.

"Hey, man. Watch where you're going, you prick," One of the crew members hollered out when their perp elbowed him out of the way. He continued running down the side of the street avoiding the site and the traffic.

Tara kept him in view. He'd removed his mask, probably to blend in and to avoid suspicion. She had an unclear view of his shadowed face when he looked back, but something about him looked familiar. She cursed out loud, knowing she wasn't gaining any ground on him. He was lean and fast. And, he seemed to know his surroundings. Where in the hell was Dobbs?

Then, she saw her partner cutting across the street in front of her, on foot. Car horns blared as he parried and swerved around the cars coming to a stop at a red light. With the stitch in her side growing in strength, she pointed and panted. "That's him a block down running like a bat out of hell. The guy in black. What is he, a damn marathon runner? He's about to piss me off." Tara dodged a drunken pedestrian weaving around the construction area.

Panting as well, Dobbs nodded toward the man they were chasing. "I see him. He's crossing over at the red light. Looks like he's circling back to 21st. He probably has a vehicle stashed around there somewhere. Let's cross here."

"The light's changing, Dobbs." Tara warned. They pulled out their badges to halt the drivers while they sprinted across the street. Pedestrians quickly moved out of the way.

They saw their man run into a clothing shop still open on the next block over. Tara and Dobbs held their guns to their sides as they followed the perp into the two-story building. They flashed their badges to the man behind the counter. Quickly searching each aisle of women's lingerie, they encountered two younger women picking through the racks. Seeing Tara and Dobbs' guns, they skittered away. Their culprit was nowhere to be seen.

Walking up to the counter, she asked the wide-eyed man, "Did you see a man dressed in black come through here?"

The man of Indian descent nodded and chattered angrily in his own language. He pointed to the back of the store. "Ran out back entrance. He knocked over one of my clothes racks. Makes me very angry."

"So sorry. Thank you." Tara called out as she and Dobbs ran toward the back of the building. Finding the heavy metal exit door, they pushed through. Standing in the middle of the street, sucking in deep, harsh breaths of the night air, they glanced left and then right, looking for their man. No one in sight. Tara's heart sank.

Then, a motor revved. Seconds later a white Equinox came roaring down the service street, almost mowing them down as it sped by. They jumped out of the way just in time, their backs flat against the building. But, they'd lost their man.

Tara rubbed her sore backside and growled in anger. "I didn't get a good look at him, but I got the license number."

CHAPTER FOURTEEN

Tara reached for her cell phone and made a quick call into precinct to issue a BOLO. She also put in a call to Chief Haynes at his home to give him an updated report. Then, she contacted Melissa asking her to get started on running the license plate while she and Dobbs walked back to the station.

Tara knew the van was stolen from their earlier reports, but she was hoping the plates would link back to the one reported missing earlier in the day. If so, they would have actual proof that would hold up in court to link the missing vehicle to their man. When he was captured, auto theft would be added to his long line of felonies.

Adrenaline and anger still pumped through her veins. Her mind flashed through what had just happened. She'd been so close to capturing the weasel, and he'd slipped right through her fingers.

She could kick herself for not reacting quicker. Jenny's life was in jeopardy, and Tara had lost him. She needed to pound on something to release her frustrations.

Unfortunately, Dobbs was the only thing close enough and he might pound back.

Trying to slow her pace and calm her heart rate, she idly glanced into the store windows as they walked past. Her thoughts ran rampant. Hopefully, luck would be on their side and the cops on patrol would be able to spot the van.

She passed a coffee shop with a large open sign hanging on its door. Her feet skidded to a sudden halt. She swiveled around and started toward the door. "Hey, Dobbs. Come on. I'm buying."

Moments later, sitting at a back booth, Tara blew on her coffee and took a sip of pure strong, black heaven. Two sips later her mind was clear enough to catch Dobbs upon her run-in with the same man who'd taken Jenny.

"He slipped right through my fingertips, Dobbs. I had him within reach, and now he's gone."

Dobbs cradled the hot mug between his hands and shook his head. He glared across the table at her, his words clipped. "That couple probably saved your life by showing up when they did. The chances of getting yourself and the two girls away from him by yourself was slim to none."

"I had to try. You would've done the same thing."

He shook his head and his fist came down hard on the table. He looked around to make sure no one heard him and lowered his voice. "No, I would've thought of my partner who could help me. Not once did you think about leaving me a clue to find you or to stall him until you could send me a message without him knowing. I'm on speed dial, Tara. One touch of your phone and I would've heard everything and responded. We're a team, dammit. I don't even know why in the hell you were out on your own. You know he's got it out for you for rescuing those girls. He blames you and that's why he kidnapped Jenny. You know that, and yet you go off at night on your own."

Tara reached out and placed her hand over his fist. She'd done what she thought was right at the time and she knew the protocol without him telling her. Yet, she hadn't meant to upset Dobbs. "I'm sorry. I didn't mean to worry you. The coffee machine in the office wasn't working again, and I needed caffeine. I was going to get coffee for us. When he showed up, my only thought was of Jenny. You have every right to be angry. It happened so fast, but you're right. I should have found a way to contact you. Please don't be mad."

Dobbs ran his hand through his stubbled hair and sighed. "No. You're right. You wouldn't have had a chance to reach your phone or do anything else. I was just blowing off steam. I'm not mad. I was scared to death." A corner of his mouth curved up. "I kinda like having you as a partner, and I didn't want to take the time to train another one."

Tara was grateful for the quirky reprieve. "Well, that's fortunate, because I kinda like being alive and having you as a partner, too."

"Good. From now on, until we catch this guy, you don't go anywhere without me. I want to know where you are at all times. Agreed?"

"Agreed. You'll know where I'm am at all times during *this* case."

Dobbs grinned when she made her promise clear.

"It's a start. Actually, a huge leap for you. You're too damn independent for your own good." The lightness in his voice was artificial. Tara knew he wanted to scold more, but held back. He knew she couldn't be pushed too far. She was too strong for that.

"Bite me, Dobbs. You're beginning to sound like a nagging husband. Maybe your mother can find you a wife tomorrow and then you can nag all you want at home and leave me alone." Tara grinned and brought the coffee cup to her lips savoring her drink. His quick laughter eased the tense situation between them.

"I don't nag, and you know what I think about getting married. So partner, you're stuck with me. Live with it." Dobbs smirked around the lip of his coffee cup.

"You're also very bossy." Without giving him a chance for a rebuttal, she stretched out the kinks in her legs. "The caffeine is starting to kick in. I think I can function for a few more hours."

"Yeah," he said. "Me, too."

"I was thinking," she said, leaning back in her seat. "The construction crew and the store owner saw his face up close. They may've seen him around before and they might know him. Or, if anything maybe they can give us a enough information for a facial sketch composite."

"It's something to check out. The crew was loading up for the day, but I got the name of the construction company. I'll get the names of the workers and have them come into headquarters tonight if you'll deal with the store owner. Also, we need to check the cameras along 22nd. Hopefully we will see a clear profile of our man."

"Sounds like a plan."

* * *

Albert was still seething an hour later. Midnight would roll around in minutes. He'd told his wife he would only be gone a short while after dinner, using the excuse he was meeting with a co-worker to have a beer or two to unwind. But, thanks to that bitch detective, he was forced to swap vehicles again. He'd had to drive to another borough before finding the red Tahoe unlocked with the motor running in front of a convenience store. It was a newer model. He hoped he got to keep it longer than the others. Even though he'd worked at a chop shop as a teen and knew how to steal a car in two minutes max, it was so much easier when he found an unlucky fool who made it easier.

He stepped out of the car he'd parked inside the garage and removed his gloves. He wanted to go inside to make sure his wife was still asleep, but he didn't dare wake her if she wasn't. He still had work to do.

Grabbing his flashlight, he made his way to the shed behind the house. Inside, he walked across the small building until he came to a locked cabinet. One that his wife or son could not get into or would ever question him about. They wouldn't dare disturb it.

Digging for the key inside his jeans pocket, he soon had the door open. Grinning, he removed six packages tightly wrapped in brown paper bags. He knew what was inside. The best cocaine money could buy. He only bought the best and his dealer always came through with the best. He had six stops to make in the morning. At this rate, the money he'd get from the sales would put him on easy street for a while. It was about time to quit his crappy job as a butcher in the crappy, local butcher shop. It would give him more time to indulge in his pleasures. Young girls. He wouldn't tell Mary, of course. It would suit his purpose to let her think he was leaving for work every morning.

He was still pissed that the chance to grab the detective failed. If that couple hadn't come by, he'd have her in his clutches right now and making her wish she'd never messed with him. He needed the time to deal with her the way he craved and Jenny would help him.

Yes, she'd gotten away.

But, not for long.

CHAPTER FIFTEEN

Tara and Dobbs brought the construction crew and the store owner into the station. Dobbs took turns with each crew member and Tara worked on the store owner. None were too happy about being brought in at such a late hour. Actually, they were pissed. A couple of patrol officers viewed the camera's footage positioned along the streets their suspect had run down.

They came to a dead end until one of the construction workers mentioned to Dobbs he'd seen their guy several times at a local bar down the street. He said their man always sat alone, drank a couple of beers and left early, around eightyish. He never caused any trouble and minded his own business. "You might want to talk to the bartender at Chugs Bar and Grill on 3rd. He might be able to tell you more."

Dobbs got the bartender's name, thanked the worker and walked him out. He found Tara in her office working on her notes she'd gotten from the store owner.

"I have nothing. The store owner didn't recognize the guy we were chasing." She told him.

Dobbs caught her up on what he'd learned from the construction workers. "I've been in that bar before. It's only a few streets over from your apartment. I think we need to check it out."

Tara nodded, her eyes drooping. "Let's go."

* * *

A few minutes later, Dobbs drove into the bar's dark parking lot. At a quarter after one on a Wednesday morning, only a couple of cars still sat on the gravel in front of the bar. The place would be hopping on the weekend, though. The Chugs was a popular place for the college kids and the younger drinking age crowd. They also catered to the business suits and the blue collars. The rock bands that alternated with the latest country bands played on the weekends, drawing them all in, keeping all of their customers happy and drinking.

A couple exited the bar as Tara and Dobbs entered. The room was empty except for another couple who sat drinking their beer and snacking on nachos and shrimp while they chatted with the young male bartender, who had long, shiny black hair, straight white teeth and cute dimples. His muscles bulged as he wiped down the counter.

They were watching a football game on the large TV mounted on the wall. Loud music played in the background. An empty polished, wooden dance floor with dim lights flickering from the ceiling was laid out directly across from the bar. Several booths and tables filled the rest of the room. The blonde waitress, who looked like she should be in junior high instead of serving drinks in a bar, sat at a nearby table texting someone on her phone.

Tara and Dobbs walked to the bar and showed the bartender their I.D. "Can we speak to you in private for a moment?" Tara asked.

The bartender glanced from the television to her and Dobbs. With a questioning look, he shrugged. "Sure." He pointed to the end of the long bar. "We can talk over there."

Following him Tara and Dobbs sat down on the bar stools facing the bar. The bartender asked, "What's this all about, Detectives?"

Tara spoke up. "We're investigating a case, and we need your help in identifying someone. We were told the man we're looking for may frequent this bar. We were hoping you could help us. What's your name?"

The bartender, still looking on edge, answered. "I'm Brad. Sure, I'll help if I can. We have so many customers coming and going that I really don't pay much attention to most, but I'll tell you what I can."

Dobbs nodded. "I understand. Maybe you'll remember this guy. We were told our guy comes in often during the week and sits at a booth alone, usually leaving around 8:00, almost on the dot. He's around six-foot-two, maybe one-hundred-eighty or ninety pounds, dark, short hair, blue eyes. Probably late thirties, somewhere in there. Do you remember seeing anyone like that in here?"

Brad thought for a moment and nodded. "Yeah. I think I remember seeing someone like that. But, Tonya our waitress would know more about him. She's usually his server. He glanced Tonya's way and got her attention with a wave of his hand. "Yo, Tonya can you come here for a minute?"

Tonya shut her phone off and strolled over to where they sat. "What's up, Brad?" she asked glancing among the three.

Tara explained to the waitress who they were looking for and gave his description.

Tonya nodded, "Yeah, I think I know who you're looking for." She pointed to a small table at the back of the dimly lit room. "He usually sits at that table and drinks two beers, no more, no less. And, then he leaves."

Tara glanced at Dobbs with a flicker of excitement gathering. "Has he ever told you his name or where he lives?"

"No, but he mentioned his son. Let me think." She snapped her fingers. "Yeah. I think he said Tommy, maybe. No, wait! Timmy. Yeah, his name was Timmy. Said he had to leave so he could get to his son's baseball game on time."

Dobbs asked, "Did he say where his son played or what league he played on?"

"I don't remember seeing him here this week, but last Tuesday, I think. Yes, last Tuesday, he said it was a home game out at Coleman Field."

Tara grinned, her thoughts whirling with hope. "That's something we can work with. We can easily find out who played there last Tuesday. Thank you so much. You don't know how much help you've been to us."

"What did this guy do?" Tonya asked.

Tara glanced into their eyes, her voice cold. "He kidnapped several teen girls. One is personal. She is my next door neighbor."

"Oh man. That's harsh. We hope you catch the guy," Tonya said.

"Yeah, good luck," Brad told them.

"Thanks. One other thing. If he comes back in here, call us right away. But, stay away from him. He's dangerous." Dobbs warned, handing them a business card.

They left the bar and walked back to the car. Climbing into the passenger seat, Tara buckled up and leaned her head against the head rest.

Dobbs glanced her way as he buckled up. "I know what you're going to say, but I'm going to suggest it anyway. It's almost two a.m. and there's nothing else we can do without waking people out of a sound sleep. Why don't we head home for a few hours and a shower? We can meet back up at around 8:00 in the morning and start fresh. What do you say? We can't help Jenny anymore tonight."

Tara looked over at him and sighed. It killed her knowing Jenny could be in worse danger or even dead. They were both exhausted and needed rest. "Yeah, you're right. Let's call it a night. We have several leads we can check out in the morning."

Dobbs nodded, too tired to smile her way. "Thank goodness. I thought you'd say 'no'." He started the car and drove out of the parking lot.

A few minutes later, Tara crawled out of the parked car in front of her apartment. She leaned into the window. "I just remembered. My car is still at the precinct. You'll have to pick me up in the morning."

"Will do. Try to get some rest, will ya?"

"Yes, Mother." Tara grinned and waved as he drove off. She walked inside her building and trudged upstairs to her apartment hoping Jake was still awake. It seemed like days instead of hours, since she'd seen him last.

Unlocking the door, she entered and walked straight to the bedroom, undressing as she went. The bed was empty. Frowning she checked the bathroom. Then, in only her underwear and shoes she made her way to the kitchen. No Jake. Glancing around the room she finally spotted a note propped against the toaster. She picked it up. It read in his scribbled hand, *Hon, had to fly to Chicago to look at some art for the studio. Be back Wednesday night. Call me if you need me.* It was right to the point. No 'Love you, Babe.' Nothing.

Disappointed, Tara filled a glass with tap water and drank it while leaning against the counter. She blew off her worry and thought about her negligee. "Lord, that sheer negligee will come in handy Wednesday night. I've got a lot of making up to do." Thinking about what would happen when Jake saw her in her newest, sexy nightwear sent a shiver of excitement through her.

Yawning, Tara placed her glass in the dishwasher and headed for the shower. Fifteen minutes later, she was in bed and sound asleep.

* * *

Jenny and Candace snuggled together, both shivering from fright. Jenny felt ashamed that she was thankful to have someone else there with her, knowing it might be their last night alive. She held Candace closer until they both drifted off to sleep.

CHAPTER SIXTEEN

Tara woke from a sound sleep. A strange, scratching sound jerked her wide awake. It was a faint sound, just loud enough to interrupt her sleep. Was someone in her bedroom? Watching her?

She lay still, listening, her fingers clutching the bedcovers.

Controlling her breathing, she raised up onto her elbows and glanced around, her senses working overtime. The bedroom, dark and shadowy, failed to give her a clue as to where the unusual noise had come from. Other than the normal traffic sounds outside her apartment, the frightened beating of her heart was the only sound pounding in her ears.

Maybe, she'd been dreaming. Since she'd gotten older and the horrible memories of her parents murder faded, nightmares were a rare occurrence, but they still happened when she was tired and stressed, like tonight. And, she didn't have Jake to massage the nightmares away.

Glancing at her alarm clock she noticed it was only 5:00 A.M. Much too early to be awake. She'd slept less than three hours. Her eyes were gritty and she felt her lids closing again from exhaustion.

Scratch.... Scratch.... Scratch.... Scraaaaaaaatch!

Her eyes jerked wide open.

There it was again. The noise sounded like it was coming from the front door of her apartment.

A metal on metal scraping.

Unless Jake made a quick round trip in one day, which was very unlikely, someone was trying to get inside her front door. Someone without a key. Or, it could be coming from the young neighbor who lived down the hall. It wasn't unusual for her to come home late after a night of weekday partying. But, she was familiar with those sounds. Not this one.

The scratching sound continued.

No. It was definitely coming from her door.

Climbing out of bed as quietly and as quickly as she could, Tara threw one of Jake's t-shirts over her underwear and reached for her pistol lying on the nightstand. Using one hand to gain her bearings, she slipped out of her bedroom and walked down the short hallway, glancing into each room. A nightlight led her way.

With her gun held in firing position with one fist over the other, she crept toward the entryway and listened. A moment later, still nothing. The front door remained closed and it was eerily silent on the other side.

Just in case someone was out there, like the perp who'd tried to nab her earlier, she yelled, "Who's there? I'm warning you, I have a loaded gun and I'm a police detective. You're breaking into the wrong apartment, asshole. If you step inside, I'll use it." And, then I'll have you, you crazy bastard.

Nothing. If someone had been outside her door, they must have heeded her warning and left. She listened a moment longer and her stance relaxed.

Tara lowered her gun and felt her heart rate slow to normal. She gave a little laugh at her own expense. The creep who'd attacked her earlier must have spooked her more than she'd realized. Now, she was hearing monsters in every corner. She checked her door lock just to be sure. Yep. It was still locked.

Tara was now wide awake and knew she wouldn't be able to go back to sleep. Feeling a little foolish, she made her way to the kitchen and put on a pot of strong coffee before heading to the shower. She'd probably heard a mouse gnawing on something. If she'd seen it, she'd probably have shot it with her nerves as rattled as they were. She could see herself explaining why she had a missing bullet to Chief Haynes.

It was a good thing Dobbs wasn't around to see her. She'd never hear the last of it. Tara Woods, a tough detective spooked by a little noise and her wild imagination. He would call her a wuss for sure.

She'd be listening for noises the rest of the morning if she tried to go back to sleep. She might as well get an early start by getting a shower and then booting up her computer while she waited on Dobbs to pick her up. She could look up local baseball teams playing at Coleman Field for the past week while she drank her coffee. Then, they along with Jackson and a couple more officers could spend the morning contacting the players and coaches of each team until they found their guy. Using the bartender and waitress

TANGLE WITH TARA

from The Chugs to identify him out of a lineup of coaches will speed things up for them.

"Sounds like a plan to catch our man," she mumbled to herself as she turned on her coffee pot. She was antsy to get to the precinct and get started. They had a good lead, but they needed more. And, Jenny needed her.

Walking into her bedroom, Tara laid her gun back down on her night stand and crossed the room to her closet. Looking inside, she pulled out a blue, pullover blouse and a pair of comfortable jeans and shoes in case she had to chase someone, again. Lord, she hoped not. She was too exhausted for any more marathons with slime balls.

She smelled the foul odor of chloroform behind her before she heard anything. The wet rag was pressed hard over her mouth and nose.

Tara reacted with trained instinct and slammed her elbow into her assailant's stomach. But, it was too late. The large hand held it firm. She had the brief satisfaction of hearing him grunt before her bare foot came down hard on top of his and then she kicked out behind her. Not connecting with hard flesh, she dropped to the floor to throw him off balanced. But, his grip only grew tighter. In desperation, her arms flailed around as she slung clothes and hangers at his head.

Light-headed, her thoughts unclear, she struggled until the strong chemical took effect and she knew no more.

CHAPTER SEVENTEEN

At 7:30 Wednesday morning, Dobbs pulled up in front of Tara's apartment building to pick her up for work. His fingers tapped on the steering wheel, his mind whirling with the little evidence they had on the case.

He glanced out the side window. Where was she? Glancing at his watch, he waited five more minutes thinking she would come be-bopping out to the car as usual. When she didn't he called her cell phone number.

She didn't answer.

Disconnecting, he tried Jake. No answer there, either.

Growing impatient, he grumbled to himself about women taking their sweet time getting ready. For him, a shower and a shave and he was out the door. Giving up on waiting, he stepped out of the car and walked up the stairs to her apartment. Maybe, she'd overslept, he conceded as he arrived at her door. She needed the rest. In that case, she would be forgiven. He grinned. She would probably tell him what he could do with his unwanted forgiveness. She was too tough to be pitied.

Dobbs raised his fist to knock, but stopped mid-way. Instead, he stepped back. His hand reached inside his vest and he pulled his revolver from its holster. The door was slightly ajar and he noticed deep scratches around the three door locks. Scratches he knew from his own training and experience had been made by someone attempting to pick the locks. The marks were too deep to come from a key. Whoever had done it knew what he was doing and had the right equipment, or he would've failed entry with the safety locks Tara had installed.

His heart began to race. He surged forward but, his fear for Tara made him hesitant and cautious. With one hand gripping his gun handle, he used his other to ease the door open wider and glanced inside.

Not seeing anyone and not daring to call out her name, he stepped into the entryway and then into the living room, his gun swinging to each corner of the room. His gaze took in every detail before giving it an all clear.

Leaving the living room, he walked with guarded steps into the kitchen and did the same. He glanced around the room looking for any obvious clue of Tara's whereabouts. Fierce, combative adrenaline rushed through his body even when his senses told him the apartment was empty other than himself. The stillness lay heavy throughout the rooms.

In the kitchen, he noticed a full pot of coffee sitting on the counter. It was luke-warm when he touched the glass with the back of his hand. A note left by Jake lay next to the coffeepot. Her notebook, mail and keys were tossed onto the kitchen table. Not wanting to contaminate what could possibly be a crime scene, he left everything lying where it was and pulled a pair of gloves from his pocket.

He still needed to check the bedroom and bathroom before calling Chief Haynes.

Just in case.

He stood in the doorway and glanced around the small room. A street light seen through the curtained window overlooking the parking lot illuminated the room. Tara's service revolver and cell phone lay on her night stand. Clothes, still on the hangers, were scattered on the closet and bedroom floor. The rug was pushed up against the foot of the bed. Small drops of blood were scattered near her closet.

She had struggled.

The blood looked almost dry from where he was standing, so it must have happened around one or two hours before. The investigators would be able to tell him more when they got there. The question was, who's blood was it? Hopefully, her assailant's. Tara would've fought him with every weapon she had within reach, including her teeth and nails if she were able.

A small smeared trail was visible across the wood floor. He hadn't noticed any blood in any of the other rooms. She must have been picked up and carried out, which meant she was unconscious, or worse. He knew in his gut she along with her assailant was long gone.

He rubbed his hand across the top of his head and sighed. Chief Haynes and CSI would need to be called in. Without a doubt, Tara's apartment was a crime scene.

Dobbs didn't venture further into the bedroom where the critical evidence was located, instead he went to the bathroom with his gun raised. Glancing through the doorway, he sighed a breath of relief.

At least, he hadn't found her deceased body. He still had a chance to find her alive.

CHAPTER EIGHTEEN

Tara's head pounded. Her battered body hurt. She glanced down to access her injuries. Whether anything was broken or not, she hurt too bad to tell. Harsh, shallow breaths pushed painfully through her sore throat and split lip. A nasty, metallic taste made her nauseous. She swallowed hard several times to keep down the bile rising in her throat.

But, she was alive.

Weak and groggy, she struggled to fight away her clouded thoughts from the chloroform gasses. She wanted nothing more than to sleep for hours. Her heavy eyes drifted shut for a couple of seconds. She jerked them wide open. She couldn't give in. Think.

She had to think.

Concentrating hard, Tara pieced together the details from the attack, but everything afterwards drew a blank. Where was she? How long had she been knocked out? A small beam of sunlight coming from a small window above warmed her skin, so she knew it was at least daylight. But, what day? Most importantly, where was *he*? A noise had awakened her. Was he still here? Watching her?

Waiting to kill her?

She tried to raise her head, but the pain shot through her skull. Moaning, she rubbed her forehead to ease her increasing headache and growing concern, but couldn't. Struggling to sit up to get her bearings, she fell back to her side. Looking down, she realized why. Her hands and feet were bound together in front of her with one short length of heavy chain, held together with a heavy lock held her in a fetal position.

Tara closed her eyes in angry frustration. She might never be able to free herself. Dammit, she wouldn't give up without trying with everything in her. Too many people were depending on her to break this case, and she wasn't about to become a crime statistic. He couldn't win.

She jerked the chains hard and cursed when the links bruised her wrists. A sharp rock beneath her dug into her hip. Scooting as far away from the rock as she could, she noticed for the first time that she was still in Jake's t-shirt and her underwear. She felt a breathtaking moment of relief. Her clothes were still on. One fear was laid to rest.

"Tara? Tara, wake up. Please, wake up. You've got to help us." The silent pleas penetrated her thoughts.

She looked toward the sound and saw Jenny and another girl watching her from across the room, chained to the wall, just as she was. Tears streaked the dirt and dried blood on their faces. Other than that and being scared to death, they seemed to be all right, physically.

Thank God.

Tara had to lick her dry lips before she could speak. "Are you two okay?"

Jenny nodded. "Yeah, for now. "

"Is he anywhere around?"

"No. After dumping you and Candace in here, and leaving bowls of food and water, he's stayed away. Yours is sitting beside your feet."

Tara looked and saw the dirty water and food in bowls just like she'd seen in front of the six girls less than twenty-four hours before. She'd have to be a lot thirstier than she was right now before drinking that nasty stuff. She glanced at the girl sitting beside Jenny and recognized her from her photo. "So, you're Candace?"

The girl nodded. "Yes ma'am. Are my parents okay? Did he hurt them?"

"No. Other than being scared and worried half to death because you're missing, they're fine. They're searching everywhere for you two along with Jenny's mom. "

Jenny's shoulder bumped her friend's in support, attempting to stay strong for her. "Now there are three of us. I don't understand what's going on, Tara. Why did he kidnap you? Why us and what is he going to do to us?"

Tara wouldn't tell them the gory details, just give them enough information to hopefully stop an overflow of panicky questions. She had too many questions and crazy thoughts of her own.

On one hand, she was in this hell-hole and hopefully can save the girls. On the other hand, she was also captured. But, she is the adult. She is the Detective.

And, she was screwed.

They all were if she didn't come up with a plan before the creep returned.

"I don't know, sweetheart. Dobbs and I believe the reason you were kidnapped is because I busted the creep's last playhouse. And, rescued six girls being held hostage there. We think he took you to get back at me, and I'm here as punishment. We think he took Candace at random."

Her only consolation was that by now, Dobbs would know she'd been kidnapped, too. He and Chief Hughes would bring in reinforcements from all jurisdictions and departments. One of their own was missing. They wouldn't leave any stone unturned until they found her and the girls. She just hoped it would be sooner rather than later.

She turned back to Jenny and Candace. "Do you know where we are?"

They both shook their heads. "We were both knocked out with something smelling really nasty that he put over our nose and mouth when he brought each of us here. I think it's an old, abandoned warehouse or something," Candace told her.

Jenny looked around the room. "Looks like they might've built something here years, ago. There's some large, rusty machines in the corner over there, but I don't know what they are."

Tara looked around and decided Jenny was right. A couple of long, rusty conveyor belts looked like they'd been thrown without a care onto the cracked, concrete floor. One large machine of some type leaned precariously against a far wall. Tall, empty cabinets with the drawers pulled out, lay on their sides. She counted three rooms with damaged doors hanging halfway off the hinges, and one loading dock with double doors. Graffiti covered the four walls and used drug needles littered the floor. Tara shuddered. The smell of rat droppings was overpowering.

There were a lot of old, abandoned buildings and factories in New York City and surrounding boroughs and most were now in high demand for renovations into apartment buildings, hotels and stores. The others were mainly used as crack houses and places for runaways to hide out.

She didn't remember any nearby abandoned factories in Manhattan other than the sugar refinery, and this wasn't it, which meant he'd taken them out of his comfort zone. But, where and how far away from his usual five mile radius?

"How long have I been here?"

Jenny shrugged. "We don't have any way to tell, but probably around an hour or so."

He could've been driving for an hour or two, but in which direction? He could've driven in circles, or, he could've hidden for that long and they were only a few minutes away from home.

"Jenny, we know you were with him at the gas station and saw what happened. Did you get a good look at the guy who kidnapped you or did he say anything that might help us know where we are?"

Jenny nodded her head. Harsh tears began to run down her face. She leaned her head on Candace's shoulder, her body shuddered. "I got a good look at him. He killed a man, Tara. I saw him, and it's all my fault. I was trying to get the man's attention to help me, but the bad guy caught me. He shot that innocent man. I should've stayed quiet, but I didn't know he had a gun. I swear. I could tell the older man was dead before we took off. He is, isn't he?"

"Sh, sweetheart," Tara soothed. "It's not your fault. No one will blame you for that. You were doing what you could to survive. But, yes. The man died on the scene. I'm sorry you had to witness something like that." And, live with that picture in her mind for the rest of her life, Tara thought.

Jenny's tears still flowed. "I'll blame myself. And, I hope when they capture this douche bag, he gets the electric chair for all the pain he's caused so many people."

Candace nodded. "Me too. He deserves the worst that can be given."

"Sorry, but that won't happen, girls. New York no longer has the death penalty. But, life in prison will be a harsher punishment. He'll get his dues. I promise," Tara told them. Oh, yes. If she was still alive when all this was over, he would suffer for what he'd done. If not, Dobbs would make sure the creep went down. She could count on him.

While she talked trying to assure the girls, she looked around the warehouse, hoping to find some means to escape. The chains were unbreakable, and she was pretty sure the door was padlocked on the outside even if they did get free. Their only choice was to wait until he came back and try to overpower him. For now, she would rest, get her strength back. She'd need every ounce inside her to take him down..

Exhausted, the girls had quieted and watched her. Tara rested her head on her arm. Just as eyes began to drift shut again, she heard the car motor and the gravel crunching beneath the tires. He was back.

CHAPTER NINETEEN

Dobbs and Chief Haynes stood in front of the officers and special crime units in the war room. Knowing they were running out of time, he filled them in on what they knew so far about the man they believed had Tara. Which wasn't much.

"Last night, the guy tried to kidnap Tara on the street, but she overtook him and he fled. We gave chase, but he got away from us. During the pursuit, he knocked against a construction worker and fortunately the worker recognized him as someone he'd seen at a local bar they both frequented. When we questioned the bartender and the waitress, we were told the guy mentioned he coached his son's baseball team not far from the bar, at Coleman Field. I have Melinda checking out the teams, coaches and visiting coaches. We'll need a team to check them and their families out. Jackson, I need you to lead this team. I don't have to tell you how vital it is to get the info back to us as quickly as possible."

Chief Haynes glanced around the room taking everyone in. "I want the rest of you to start knocking on Tara's neighbors' doors. At that hour of the morning, it's doubtful anyone saw or heard anything, but we need to ask. Detectives, I need you to work with all available agencies.

Check out their databases. Get me a list of all released convicted felons living within a ten-mile radius of where the girls were taken and Tara's apartment. Check the jail records. This creep may have flown under the radar his entire life, but, we may luck out. Let's find him."

Detective Haynes dismissed the group. Before they could file out of the room, they were stopped when Melinda rushed into the room waving several print outs.

"I've got the list." Melinda handed the sheets to Dobbs and passed out copies to the others. "There are six names, all coaches. All six have sons playing this baseball season and all six live within the five-mile radius." She grinned, looking very pleased. "But, look at number three. He lives one block over from both Tara and Jenny and not far from Candace."

Dobbs and Chief Haynes grinned. "Good job, Melinda. Okay guys. We know where to start our search," Dobbs said.

Jackson stood still as the others were leaving. He tapped his finger against the sheets in his hand. "I know this address. The wife was one of the neighbors we questioned when that Candace girl came up missing. The husband was at work when we were there, so he wouldn't have seen or heard anything." He shook his head. "After seeing this list, I have a gut feeling he won't be home this time, either."

* * *

Chief Haynes paced his office, his hands clenched. Dammit, he felt helpless. There were still things he could do, things he needed to do. He reached for his phone and began calling in extra favors to the local and state agencies and the Federal Bureau as well as the media. Tara was like a daughter to him and he would bring her home safe. He had to.

Then, he put in the dreaded phone call to Jake. With his voice shaken, he told Dobbs he was flying home as soon as he could get a flight out. Tara would be pissed at him for worrying Jake. But, dammit. The man shared her bed and her life. He deserved to know.

* * *

When Dobbs stepped through the doors of the precinct mic's or phones from all branches of the media was shoved into his face. Damn, they worked fast. The Chief had notified them less than a half an hour ago and warned Dobbs he would be expected to give the reporters a full report on any information that wouldn't compromise the investigation.

Dobbs told the familiar faces of television, radio, and newspaper journalists everything the police department could give them at this time. He handed out pictures of Tara to go along with the photos they had been running since yesterday on the two missing girls. He wanted their faces in front of everyone hoping someone knew or had seen something. Moments later, Dobbs ended the questions and hurried to his car.

Several minutes later, he pulled up behind Officer Jackson's patrol car in front of the Jones' home. Walking up to the suspect's home, he nodded to a young officer standing at the doorway as he entered and strode through the room toward the sound of voices. Entering the kitchen, he saw Jackson sitting at the kitchen table, a middle-aged woman across from him nervously picking at a string loose on a cloth napkin. A young boy in his early teens sat next to her. Jackson showed the pictures of Tara, Jenny and Candace. "Mrs. Jones. I know we've questioned you when Candace went missing, and you weren't able to help us. I'm wondering if you know the detective who lives down the street, or maybe Timmy knows Jenny. They're near the same age?"

The woman glanced at the pictures. Her brows drew together as she thought for a moment. Then she nodded as she recognized Tara. "Yes, I've seen her around the neighborhood. I've always thought how safe I felt knowing a detective lived nearby. I think I've seen the girl, but I'm not sure where. Timmy do you know her?" She passed the picture of Jenny across the table to her son.

He glanced at the picture and nodded. "Yes, I've seen her at school. We have a couple of classes together, but she doesn't hang out with the nerds, so we're not friends. I just know her name." He smirked and handed the picture back to Jackson. "It's not like we hang out or anything."

Dobbs glanced at the boy. No, he didn't see this Timmy and Jenny hanging out. There was something about the boy that raised his hackles. And, he didn't believe it was a coincidence that the name of the boy the waitress gave and the boy now sitting at the table was both named Timmy. No way in hell.

Turning away from them, he half-listened in on the questioning, while looking around the room in hopes of seeing any type of evidence to tie Jones to the kidnappings and homicides.

TANGLE WITH TARA

He noticed the kitchen was small and the appliances and decor were outdated, but everything was scrubbed clean and organized. He could tell the kitchen was the center of their family's life. A baseball bat stood in one corner with a catcher's mitt draped over it.

He glanced back at Jackson and then took a few steps further to see into the other rooms. A family portrait hung on the living room wall, visible from the kitchen doorway. The man in the picture looked very much like the description they'd gotten from the woman at the gas station. A long, white cover up jacket hung on a coat rack just inside the door leading to the laundry room. Walking over to the jacket, Dobbs noticed the words Paddy's Butcher Shop embroidered on the front pocket. Dark, red blood stains covered the front. Bingo. He'd found the uniform he'd earlier guessed the perp wore. Coincidence? Hell no. He just hoped it wasn't Tara's or one of the girl's blood. He tuned back into the conversation.

Jackson asked. "Mrs. Jones. Can you tell me your husband's whereabouts yesterday?"

The woman's hands shook as she pushed back the dark hair from her face. She glanced over at her son and then back to Jackson. "Albert, my husband, had to work overtime and didn't get home until around eight last night. We ate dinner while Timmy told him about the baseball game he had to miss. After dinner, Albert was trying to make up to Timmy for missing the game again, so, they spent some bonding time together while I cleaned the kitchen. After that, we went to bed. Albert had to be at work early this morning and was gone before I got up. He hasn't come home, yet."

"Do you know if you're husband left the house any time after you went to bed?" Dobbs asked.

She shook her head. "He wouldn't have any reason to, would he?"

"I don't know. That's why I'm asking you."

She shrugged, looking embarrassed, her voice just above a whisper. "My husband insists that I take a sleeping pill every night, so I won't be restless and keep him awake. So, no. I couldn't tell you for certain that he didn't leave. A bomb could go off after I take the pill and I wouldn't hear it. But, I really don't understand why you're asking me these questions. What does any of this have to do with the three missing girls?"

Timmy stood up. The small round table scooted from the force of his movement. With his hands clenched tightly at his side, he yelled. "You think my Dad has something to do with them going missing, don't you? My Dad wouldn't do anything like that. He's a good man. You're suspecting the wrong person." His voice rose, his face blood-red. His eyes shone from the tears he wouldn't allow to fall. "Tell them, Mom. They're wrong. Tell them. Mom, they think he did it!"

"It's okay, son. Timmy's right, officer. My Albert would never do anything that horrific. He's a good hard-working man. Besides, if he's not at work, he's at home with us or at the baseball field with Timmy."

Dobbs piped in. He pointed to where the white jacket hung. "Is Paddy's Butcher Shop his only employment?"

"Yes. He puts in plenty enough of overtime there that he doesn't need to work anywhere else." She looked pointedly at Jackson. "Nor, would he have the time to do anything else."

Jackson stood without responding, and handed the woman his card. "Ma'am, if you see or hear from your husband, ask him to call us. We have some questions for him and we want answers." He glanced hard at the wife and son before placing his hat on his head and walked out. Dobbs followed.

Outside, Jackson turned to Dobbs. "I could tell the wife knew nothing about what her husband could be doing while she sleeps. My gut is telling me he kidnapped and killed those girls. Those two in there are just more innocent victims. We still don't have the proof we need to arrest this guy. "

Dobbs nodded. "I'm with you, Jackson. We'll find that proof."

Jackson nodded back and headed down the steps. "You damn right we will, Dobbs."

Dobbs stood beside his car. He glanced at his watch. It showed 10:30. The time was flying by too fast. "Meet me at the precinct. I want to give Chief Haynes a short briefing on what we found out, then let's check out this Paddy's Butcher Shop. I want to know what his employer says about him."

Jackson nodded and opened his cruiser door. "Let's go. We're wasting daylight. He has Tara."

* * *

An hour later, Dobbs parked in an empty spot in front of the local butcher shop. A large, bright, crackling neon sign with just enough letters lit up to know it read Paddy's Butcher Shop blinked above the store front. The front window had one small round hole with spider web cracks in the pane from either a thrown rock or in this neighborhood it was most likely from a bullet. Fingerprints spotted the rest of the glass. Paper blown from the sidewalk lay flat against the glass front door. A large "OPEN" sign hung on the inside.

Dobbs glanced at Jackson to see if his reaction was the same as his. It was. Not exactly a place of business where he would want to buy butchered meat. He wondered how often the Health Board inspected this place.

He turned the wobbly door knob and walked inside with Jackson following. A man with curly, red hair and a long beard stood behind the counter where cut meat was displayed in one section and deli meat and cheese in the other. Evidently, the man used his white jacket as a rag after cutting the meat. The front was a bloody mess. But, other than that, the place was sparkling clean which surprised the heck out of Dobbs.

The man smiled at his customers as they approached the counter. "A good morning to you, gentleman. What can I get you?"

Dobbs pulled out his badge. "Information. Are you the owner?"

With a puzzled look, the man glanced from Dobbs to Jackson and back to Dobbs. "Yes sir. I am."

"I understand that an Albert Jones works for you. Is he working today?"

Paddy snorted. "That sorry, good-for-nothing hasn't showed up for work in two days. He does this to me over and over, leaving me short-handed. But, because of his sweet wife, which I've met only once, I let him keep his job every time. Not this time. I'm tired of the way he does me. When he comes in, I'm letting him go. I need someone I can rely on. Why? What has that sorry son of a bitch done, now?"

Dobbs ignored the question. "Do you know if he has another job other than here?"

"Not a clue. He just shows up when he wants to and begs me not to tell his wife or son he hadn't been to work. Of course, he always tells me it won't happen again. Lying sucker."

"What about his co-workers? Would they know anything?"

Paddy pinched his bottom lip while he thought. "Nah. I don't think Johnny or Sam have much to do with him. They're not buddy buddy, if you know what I mean? They didn't share a lunch table in the breakroom. So, I don't think Albert would share any secrets with them. "

Deflated and running out of ideas, Dobbs nodded and slid a card across the counter. "If he comes in, give me a call. Whatever you do, don't anger him. We think he may be very dangerous and possibly armed. Just walk out of the room and call us. Okay?"

Dobbs and Jackson left the shop while the owner was too shocked to ask any more questions.

CHAPTER TWENTY

Albert still sat in his minivan, hidden a block away from his home contemplating his future. Earlier, he'd watched the officers and the detective enter his house and then leave a few minutes later. A satisfied grin appeared. If they'd shown up five minutes later, they would've caught him at home. Luckily, he saw them before they saw him.

He'd recognized the detective walking up to his front door. He was the partner of the vile woman he now held captive. Albert almost laughed in glee. The detective would never find his partner alive.

He wasn't worried about his family telling the police anything about his secret life no matter how rattled they got. They didn't know anything. Didn't suspect anything. Even, if they did, they wouldn't snitch him out.

But, the time to move on had finally come. He couldn't take the chance the cops would put all of the pieces together. He knew if he stayed around, they would find and capture him, sooner or later. He couldn't survive being captured, again.

It wounded him heart and soul that he would have to leave his wife and son behind. They'd built a wonderful, loving life together. There wasn't any other option. He couldn't stand the thought of his beloved family finding out his secrets. It would kill them. And, he wouldn't put them on the run. He couldn't take the chance they would start asking too many questions and get suspicious if he took them with him. They deserved a better life than what he could give them if he took them with him.

He'd planned for this. He'd prepared.

They had no other family to take them in, but they would be taken care of even after he was gone. He made sure of it.

He'd put enough money from his crappy job at the butcher shop in the bank so that his wife and son would be well taken care of when he left. They would also have the half-million dollars from the life insurance policy he'd bought a year back, after the insurance company paid out for his untimely death.

From his drug sales over the last several months, he had enough money to live well in Mexico for years to come. So what if he had to go from blonde-haired girls to dark-haired? He could adjust.

Even back then he was planning. He already had his plane ticket bought.

Albert realized he might be on a suicide mission if his plans failed, but no way could he be imprisoned like he was when his mother chained him downstairs. Never. Never. Never.

He would kill again and again if it would keep him free.

Oh, yes. His family would miss him. But, they would miss him if he was thrown into the pen for life.

At least this way, his Mary and Timmy would be able to hold their head high if he just came up missing or pronounced dead. They would take care of his dog. They would move on with his memory. They would forget him sooner or later. And, they would be well taken care of in the future. Without him. That was all that mattered to him.

He had a fail-proof, easy peasy plan, he thought. The Fire Commissioner would find a body about his size wearing his ring and watch in Paddy's Butcher Shop after he burned the building to the ground. By the time the ashes cooled, the body would be burned beyond recognition. All they would have would be his jewelry to identify him. He hated that damn shop. Too bad he couldn't stick around to watch the bastard Paddy's face as the building burned. He already had the poor victim picked out to take his place in the fire. He'd been scouting out the homeless that hung around the neighborhood. There was one who was the perfect size and toothless about four blocks away from the butcher shop. He was nothing to humanity, just an expendable drunk. No one would miss him and they wouldn't be able to use his dental records for identity.

After a few minutes of them entering his home, he'd watched the cops and detective file out the front door, glancing around as if they might see him walking up. "Not happening, suckers," He muttered.

Yet, he'd allowed them to get too close. They'd talked to his family and touched his things without his permission. His fist clenched .

Anger fueled through him. He slapped his hand against the steering wheel. His eyes narrowed and he slapped it again. His foot pressed hard against the floorboard.

Everything was all that detective's fault. "Damn her to hell and back."

If she hadn't messed with his little girls and pissed him off, he'd be going about his enjoyable daily life, the same way he had for years, without the threat of being caught. He loved the routine he'd established. He hated her for causing him to lose his family and the home he'd live in for all his life. She would pay dearly. If he couldn't have a future with his family, she couldn't have a life.

Tonight, she would meet her maker.

But, first he had things to do. Preparations to make. Things to buy.

Tonight.

Tomorrow, he'd be gone.

CHAPTER TWENTY ONE

Two hours later, Dobbs hit the 'end call' button after hearing news that didn't make his day get any better. A couple of officers reported they'd checked out all of the hospitals and morgues in Manhattan and the surrounding boroughs with no luck. No one by the name of Albert Jones or a John Doe with his description had been brought in to either facility. He was alive and unhurt. They'd searched all of the known places he frequented, including the baseball field and local bar. He had not returned home or to work. He was nowhere to be found.

Albert Jones had disappeared.

One thing Dobbs felt in his churning gut. Find him and he would find Tara and the girls.

* * *

The metal lock on the dock doors rattled hard. Rap music boomed from a vehicle's stereo. The old warehouse walls vibrated with each beat.

The two girls, who had relaxed very little in the last hour or so drew themselves into a tight balls, almost as if they were trying to make themselves disappear. Tara whispered encouragement. "It's going to be okay. Keep your eyes on me at all times for my directions. If I tell you to act, I need you do it right then. Do not hesitate. Understand?" She waited for their nod and braced for their abductor to enter. She would have to act, take him by surprise when the opportunity came her way. She was ready.

The lock rattled again.

Jerked.

Rattled.

Tara heard cussing, over several raised voices talking at once. Then, the footsteps grew faint on the gravel and the voices grew dimmer.

They were leaving! "Help! Help us!" She screamed at the top of her lungs. The girls joined in, yelling for all they were worth All she heard was an engine start up and the gravel crunching beneath the tires as the vehicle drove away. It wasn't their kidnapper.

Tara cursed as she realized they might have missed their only chance to escape. Never mind that the visitors were probably looking for their usual safe haven to do their drugs, or sell them. The needles she saw on the floor supported her beliefs.

It was someone who knew they were far enough from the beaten path to know it didn't matter how much noise they made or to worry that anyone would catch them in the act, which also supported her theory: No one, but the druggies ever came here.

But, where in the hell was this place? And, how did their abductor find it? Tara's only hope was that the visitors would come back with a lock cutter. She wouldn't hold her breath, though.

Glancing toward the girls, Tara noticed them leaning against each other, shaken, but trying to keep it together.

"Hey Jenny?"

The girl hiccupped. "Yeah?" Her fingers couldn't reach her fallen tears.

"You know Dobbs will find us, right? He's not going to stop searching until he does. I have faith in my partner and Chief Haynes. And, Jake." The thought of no future with Jake caused her stomach to clench. No, she wouldn't allow herself to think about it. She had to keep her head straight.

Jenny sank lower to the floor, her spirit seemed to be close to breaking. "I know, but will they find us dead or alive?" She lifted her shoulder, turned her face and wiped the tears against her cotton T-shirt.

"Alive, of course. Keep your faith, Jenny. Your mother and the rest of us are counting on you to be strong and fierce. You too, Candace." Tara pointed toward her own heart. "Your family, friends and God are right here in your heart with you. Hold on to that thought and never give up the fight."

"I want to, but it's so hard," Candace told her.

"We're trying, Tara," Jenny said. "And, I hate that you're here, but I'm glad you are, if you know what I mean. We don't feel so helpless and alone, anymore."

"I understand, sweetie. Just be strong. Okay?"

Jenny nodded. She glanced at Candace who nodded, as well. The fear in their eyes diminished a little.

"Good. I'm so proud of you two." Tara glanced from the frightened girls to the bowls on the floor next to her. The early morning scrambled eggs had turned to liquid and unappetizing, the bacon limp and smelly. At least the water looked clean, and she was thirsty enough to try it. With no air stirring inside, the warehouse became like a smoldering tin can. But, could he have poisoned the water? She wasn't that desperate, yet.

"Have you girls drunk the water or eaten any of the food he's put out?"

Candace nodded. "We drank and ate some earlier."

"And, you feel okay?"

"Yes. Why?"

"No drugged feeling, either of you?"

They glanced down at the bowls in horror. Both shook their heads.

Jenny swallowed hard and glanced back at Tara. "Do you think he drugged our water or food? It's disgusting, but we'll starve if we have to do without."

"It was just a thought, but since you both feel fine, I'm sure it's okay. You'd be feeling the effects if he had." Carefully, Tara picked up the water bowl with her fingertips. With only an inch to spare, she brought it to her mouth and took an experimental sip. The liquid was lukewarm, but delicious. She drank deeply, and then splashed the few drops left, onto her face. They had to keep hydrated.

She had no way of knowing when their captor would return with fresh water and food. If he did. He was crazy enough to leave them there to die. But, she had a feeling he had worse in mind.

CHAPTER TWENTY TWO

The day grew late, and Dobbs' worries increased. Eight hours earlier, Dobbs had found Tara missing, and it was close to thirty-four hours since Stacy had realized Jenny was missing.

Too damn long.

Dobbs glanced at his watch. 2:45 p.m. He tried to suppress the worry that seemed to be on the rise while Jackson drove them back to the precinct.

Entering Dobbs' office, they settled back in their chairs and went over what they knew so far. They didn't have any positive proof, but Dobbs' gut instinct kept his suspicions targeted on this Albert guy.

"This is what we have on Jones." He began counting off the list on his fingers. "Number one, he lived close to Tara and the two latest missing girls. Number two, he was a coach at Coleman's Field. Number three, his son played baseball. Number four, his boss didn't like Albert much. Number five, he drugged his wife with..., we just found out was street drugs. The evidence is starting to add up as well as the questions."

Jackson leaned back in the chair. "Why would Jones give her something that strong? Why not just an over the counter sleeping pill? Unless, he wanted to make sure his wife didn't wake up at night. But, why would he go to that extreme?"

"He couldn't take the chance she would wake up and ask questions when he returned. It's easy to know where he gets the drugs to give to his wife. A drug dealer is on just about every street corner. He can get any type of prescription meds he needs these days." The undercover drug force was snipping at the heels of the main sources and some had been busted, but there was still an abundant supply for the dealers of drugs in that area.

Dobbs would bet his next paycheck this Albert didn't work overtime, the way his wife said. From what his boss said, he was too lazy to work one job, much less two. It didn't take a rocket scientist to know he was lying to his wife. Comparing the conversations they'd had with his wife and what his boss had told them, made that pretty clear. He could easily be kidnapping the girls with no one the wiser. Living a secret, double life.

Even more importantly, why hadn't there been more bodies found? He didn't believe for one minute Albert had just started his kidnapping spree. No way were the six girls found Tuesday night his only kidnap victims. But, other than the three latest murders in that vicinity, no other bodies had been found.

Had he narrowed his killing field? Did he have more unsolved victims outside the five-mile radius they'd been concentrating on? "What in the hell is he doing with the bodies? He's not releasing his victims. They're still listed as missing. They have to be somewhere."

Jackson glanced his way. Experience had hardened the seasoned veteran. He shrugged. "Maybe he worked in other territories in his younger days and we haven't connected all the dots in our database. If he's been getting away with it for years, he may feel safe enough to bring his addiction closer to home. His wife and son are devoted to the man. Maybe he wants to have his fun and return home to his wife at least part of the night. Look at Ted Bundy. His wife didn't know what he was doing, either."

Before Dobbs could reply, his phone rang.

"Dobbs?" Melinda spoke in a rush. "Listen to this."

Dobbs stood and began to pace. "Give it to me, Melinda. Jackson is here and I have you on speaker phone."

Excitement ran through her voice. "I ran Jones's current address. He lived there at an early age and returned about seventeen years ago from Chicago, where he worked at a grocery store as a butcher. As soon as he returned to Manhattan, he bought his old house and moved in, married his current wife, and they had the one son. But, get this. I found an old newspaper article dated back twenty-five years ago. I'm emailing it to you now. It mentions a Mrs. Betty Jones who took off and left her son behind. There's a picture of Albert Jones at the age of fourteen, bruised and malnourished. His father had passed away about four years prior, so Albert was placed in foster care. But, get this. The article showed a picture of a small basement inside the house complete with chains, locks and dog bowls on the floor. Sound familiar?"

CHAPTER TWENTY-THREE

It took less than an hour for the search warrant to come through after Chief Haynes made the rushed request. Mary Jones refused them entrance into her home without one. It delayed them, but wouldn't stop them.

Fifteen minutes later, Dobbs and Jackson sped back to the Jones's home and rang the doorbell. When Mary answered the door, Jackson held out the warrant. "We'll need to search your home, particularly the basement, Mrs. Jones," he said, his voice firm.

Mary Jones looked at a closed door just down the hallway that led off of the living room. She turned and glared back at them. But, as furious as she was, she kept her voice low. "I don't know why you're trying to accuse my husband. He would never do anything wrong, especially to those girls you mentioned, earlier. He's a good man and supporter. And, he has nothing to hide down in that basement. He told me, so."

"You may be right, but we still need to take a look. If there's nothing down there, we'll move on." Always suspicious, Dobbs walked to the door Mary had glanced toward earlier. "Is your husband in here, Mrs. Jones?"

"No. My son is taking a nap, and I don't want to wake him. He's had a rough day and needs the rest."

Dobbs opened the door and peeked into a bedroom decorated in a baseball theme. Timmy lay diagonal across the bed, sound asleep. Satisfied Jones wasn't hiding out in the room, he backed out and closed the door with a soft click. Then, he went down the hall and checked the other two bedrooms, glancing into the closets as he went. The last bedroom's closet held the couple's clothes. "Mrs. Jones, do you know if any of Albert's clothes are missing?"

She stepped into the bedroom's doorway and crossed her arms over her chest. "I didn't notice any missing this morning when I washed and hung up his clothes. Only things gone are the clothes and the smock uniform he would've worn to work this morning. Everything else seems to be there."

Dobbs nodded and stepped away from the closet. They met Jackson in the hallway. "Have you talked to your husband since we were here this morning?"

She frowned. Concern showed in her eyes. "No. He's still not answering my calls. I'm growing so worried."

Dobbs tried to ease her fear. "We've contacted the hospitals and morgues. No one by his name or description has been checked in."

"Thank God for that, at least." she wiped away a runaway tear and walked back into the kitchen. Grabbing a dishrag, she began scrubbing her already clean counter.

"Mrs. Jones, we really need to see the basement now," Jackson told her with a kind, and sympathetic tone. He shifted from one foot to the other as if tearful women made him nervous.

With a hesitant nod, her shoulders drooped in surrender. She glanced back at Dobbs and Jackson and hung up the dishrag to dry. "That piece of paper you handed me won't do you any good. Albert has kept a padlock on the basement door since before we were married. I've never been in the basement."

Jackson's brow rose. "Did he say why he kept it locked?"

"Just that he has a lot of his mother's things downstairs. He didn't want anyone damaging them."

"Let's take a look." Dobbs nodded to Mrs. Jones. "Lead the way, please."

The three made their way through the kitchen and down another short hallway. Mary stopped in front of a solid steel door blocking the way to the basement stairs. A large, heavy duty lock was threaded through the latch and hasp, and the steel door had a keyed deadbolt lock.

"Do you have a key to both locks?" Dobbs doubted it since she hadn't been downstairs, but he asked anyway as he pulled on the lock.

"No. Albert keeps both sets of keys with him at all times."

Dobbs blew out a frustrated breath. "Jackson, can you grab your lock cutters out of your cruiser? We've got to cut this loose." *Dammit.* He knew it wouldn't take Jackson long. But, they didn't have the time to waste.

Jackson nodded. "Be right back."

"Now, wait a minute. Albert won't like it if you damage his door or cut his locks. He said he had to special order that door." Mary wrung her hands. She looked from Dobbs to Jackson, her red-rimmed eyes wide with fear.

"The lock cutter will be able to cut both locks without damaging the door. He can buy more locks. While we're waiting, why don't you try giving your husband another call, to see if he'll answer this time. If he does, try to get him to come home. If he won't come, try to find out his whereabouts. I'd appreciate it if you wouldn't tell him we're here. If he'd just come home and talk to us we might clear this whole mess up. Okay?"

Mary nodded, her shoulders drooped. "Let me get my phone." She walked back into the kitchen. Dobbs followed close behind her. If Jones answered, he wanted to hear the full conversation.

If he answered.

Dobbs worried that somehow Jones had found out they were on to him. The only way her husband would know is if Mary had lied about not talking to her husband when she'd called him earlier. If she'd warned her husband, he would've had time to deal with Tara and the girls and still be long gone. The thought made Dobbs' gut churn. He began pacing the floor.

Across the room, her phone rang and rang. He didn't pick up. Mary finally left him a brief message to call her and ended the call with a deep sigh. She turned her back on them and leaned against the kitchen counter. Her head lowered as if in prayer.

Jackson entered the kitchen, placing his cell phone into his shirt pocket. "Here's the cutter. I just talked to Chief Haynes. He's going to be here, shortly. Did Jones answer?"

Dobbs shook his head. "No. We can try again, later."

"Why are you messing with my mama, again? We told you my dad was innocent. Leave us alone." Timmy stood in the doorway, his fists clenched tight. His hair on one side was smashed flat from his pillow. Even in anger, he looked beaten down and hurting inside. Just like his mama.

"We just want to talk to him, son." Dobbs raised his hand in a "take it easy" gesture and then took a tentative step closer. The boy was tall and lanky, growing into his own skin. But, he could still be a threat if he started throwing punches. He looked like he wanted to, but held back. Probably for his mama's sake.

"Timmy, that's enough." His mother walked over to him and shook her finger in his face. "We did not raise you to be disrespectful. I want you to apologize to the detective and the officer. Then, go back to your room until I call you for dinner. Let us adults handle this. Understand?"

Timmy's face turned bright red, either from anger or embarrassment for being scolded in front of Dobbs and Jackson. "Yes, ma'am." He glared at them and muttered "Sorry." Then he turned and walked back to his room, slamming the door behind him.

Mary rubbed her forehead and closed her eyes for a moment. "I'm sorry. I'll talk to him later."

"We understand, Mrs. Jones. But, we have to do everything possible to find Detective Woods and those girls."

"I know. But, you need to be looking somewhere else. You're wasting your precious time here."

Before she could say anything more, they heard a car door slam outside. Mary's eyes widened. "Albert?" She hurried to the door and swung it open. A disappointed cry escaped when she saw it wasn't her husband, but instead it was from the house next door. Wearing a defeated look, she stepped back and closed the door.

With a brief nod to Dobbs, Jackson led the way to the basement.

When they reached the basement, they gave each other a 'are you ready' look before Jackson cut the locks off the door. With caution, Dobbs opened the door. Jackson reached inside and found a light switch on the wall. He flipped it and they descended. Spider webs swung from corner to corner. Dobbs had a fit of sneezing from the scattered dust they disturbed. Mary returned and followed them down the steps. They stopped at the bottom of the steps and stared in shock at the objects they saw before them.

It was *deja vu* all over again.

Sets of chains were bolted low into the paneling with open locks dangling on the two chains. Dobbs counted six sets along the four walls. Two empty, dirty dog bowls were placed in front of each one. On one side of the room a wooden door with a small window gave him the view of the back yard.

And, then he noticed one set of chains that were different. He walked over to examine them. The metal was severely pitted from rust as if it had been there for decades. The two dog bowls sitting in front of it were busted and faded. The

TANGLE WITH TARA

pictures Melinda had emailed them earlier were the before pictures. This was the after.

Dobbs glanced back at Jackson. "This is set up just like the one we found Tuesday night. He's had girls down here as well." He ignored Mary's harsh gasp and continued. "Let's see what else we can find."

The two began searching the whole basement while Mary looked on in disbelief. Dobbs quickly spotted a place in the concrete floor in one corner that was buckled in the middle and a large, wide crack snaked along the area for about four feet. "Let me see your flashlight," he told Jackson. When he had it in his hand, he beamed the light down into the crack to the dirt beneath.

Below the crack in the concrete a human skull with empty eye sockets seemed to stare back at him in horror.

CHAPTER TWENTY-FOUR

A couple of hours later, Dobbs and Jackson stood beside Chief Haynes, the FBI agent assigned to the case and the head of the forensic team inside the Jones' basement.

The five men watched as the concrete was broken up and carefully removed piece by piece for easy access to the body. When an opening was wide enough for a three man team, they took painstaking and timely care to recover the bones from the harsh, shallow burial site. After clear, concise descriptions were written, photographs and samples were taken, the remains were placed into a tagged body bag.

Without the DNA results available Dobbs could only make a guess that their discovery was the missing mother who didn't resurface fifteen years earlier. Melinda said the newspaper listed her name as Betty Jones. Albert Jones' mother.

Who killed her? Albert, her own son who had obviously been abused? Or, maybe someone else? The old newspaper clipping mentioned Albert was fourteen years old when it happened and he was placed in a foster home soon after. That didn't mean he didn't hide her elsewhere and then return days or months later to move her to her final resting place when it was safe.

Was it possible someone in town sold him the concrete and might remember Albert buying them? Or, was it already available to the son?

At his age, he could've read the directions on the bags and mixed it himself. The picture in the newspaper showed an unfinished concrete floor going about three quarters of the way across the room.

It might have been something his father started before he died. Albert could've finished pouring it off and allowed the cement to cure before the officials arrived and found him bruised and all alone. It was all a speculation, but it felt right to Dobbs.

Glancing toward one wall with tall shelves built up to the ceiling gave him his answer. Six bags of concrete lay on the bottom shelf. From the condition of the bags, they had been stored there for a very long time. Years.

Dobbs had his theories of what happened and he was certain from the damning facts they'd uncovered in the last few hours who held Tara and the girls captive. But, where were they? How were they?

Dobbs jaw clenched. A nerve pulsated in his neck as he glanced at Jackson who was still watching the removal. He motioned for Jackson to follow him out of the basement. Climbing back upstairs, into the kitchen, the two walked outside into the fresh, evening air.

Dobbs filled him in on what he believed happened to the young Albert and his deceased mother. He wanted Jackson's thoughts. "Do you think it's possible he would've had the strength to mix and pour maybe a ten by ten foot space and then get rid of the evidence? The picture showed him malnourished with bruises on his face and arms. I bet he didn't way much over eighty pounds."

Jackson leaned against the house and propped his foot back against the brick. He rubbed his chin in thought. "I think he could if the casing was already down. I don't know if he would've taken the time to build up the area. He would be rushing to get it poured over her body to give the concrete time to dry before he called the authorities."

"How much time are we talking about?"

"It usually takes about two to three days to cure and he had twenty-four to seventy-two hours before stench of her body would give him away. I think he wanted the law enforcement to believe he was abused and abandoned by allowing them to see the dog bowls and chains in the basement, but no mother."

"I think so, too. So, it's doable?"

"Yes. I figure he had many years of abuse to figure out how to pull it off."

"That's the sad part." Dobbs heard several voices growing near. Glancing up and down the street in front of the Jones' home Dobbs noticed the media vans arriving and parking behind the forensic and the coroner's vans. News traveled fast.

Damn vultures.

But, those vultures sometimes helped their case. Dobbs planned on putting their extensive contacts to good use.

* * *

TANGLE WITH TARA

By 7:30 Wednesday night, Jones' face and the stolen vehicle they believed he was still driving were plastered all over the T.V. and the social media. Special news bulletins interrupted local broadcasts announcing a reward offered for anyone who could help them apprehend their latest suspect.

Phones were ringing off the hook at the precinct with people calling in with possible leads. Some didn't pan out, but a few were worthy of checking out.

The last sighting was on I-495. The person calling in was driving beside a S.U.V. who he believed was the suspect in the next lane. His passenger snapped pictures of the driver and the license plate. They immediately sent the pictures to the 13th precinct. It was Jones. Finally, luck was on their side.

The officers went into action putting patrol cars in place along the highway. They'd warned the driver calling in to back off to a safe distance. Jones was considered armed and dangerous.

* * *

The warehouse grew darker and the floor colder. The evening sun dipped low in the sky. The small window above marked its slow progress.

Tara's wrists were bleeding from trying to loosen them from chains, to no avail. She and the girls were still bound.

Jenny and Candace had fallen into an exhausted sleep around an hour before. She had no way of telling the time other than the sun's gradual descent in the window and knew it would be totally dark, soon.

Tara's head still pounded from the chloroform. They hadn't eaten or drank anything since earlier that morning. She was exhausted and she'd nodded off several times, but every slight noise woke her.

Her weary mind came up with only one solution. She had to overtake him when he unchained her. She was more than capable under normal circumstances. Nothing about this was normal. She knew she needed to be rested to accomplish anything that drastic.

She had all of the confidence in the world her partner would find them. Until then, using her strength and her wits remained her only chance to get herself and the girls safely away from this maniac.

She'd overpowered him before. She could do it again. But, if she didn't find the much needed strength this time, the three would die.

CHAPTER TWENTY-FIVE

Doogie and Popmaster each hugged a half-dressed girl against their side. All four were doubled over with laughter stimulated by the liquor. They passed a rolled joint back and forth between them causing their flashlights to jerk erratically in front of them.

Pot and Jack Daniels straight were their choices so far that night. They were waiting to get inside their hideout to do the serious shit.

It was nine-thirty at night and no one other than their friends would come around this late. It didn't matter to his friends what time it was. When they came off of their high, they would show up either day or night needing another buzz. Sometimes as many as twenty or thirty in a group or as less as two or three friends would party with them at any given time.

The rundown plant was their private sanctuary when they wanted to use the needles and relax the night through in a daze. The place hadn't been raided by the drug force in a while. Hell, they'd left their stash of condoms and needles stored everywhere and the dumb, lazy cops still hadn't caught them.

Not that the cops spent much time looking. They had bigger fish to fry than the small time heroin users. Like murders and rapist and such shit. Doogie wasn't scared of no Copper. At that thought, he laughed even harder. Copper. He'd been watching too many old Spencer Tracy movies with his grandfather.

Doogie brought his thoughts back to the surroundings and glanced down at the girl rubbing against him and winked.

He knew he was a good-looking kid and was fun to be around. He used it to his advantage. He was the lead captain of his high school football team. His long, black hair falling below his shoulders, his dark, midnight, come-hither eyes and his athletic build guaranteed him any girl he wanted.

Whereas, Popmaster was as dumb as a rock and built like a 6 foot pit bull. As the defense on the football team, he knocked his opponents out like a bowling ball, a steam roller. He didn't get his earned nickname without a reason. His hard hits usually popped the unlucky opponent right out of the game.

But, unlike Doogie, Popmaster's scarred face, broken nose and bald head made it harder for him to find a girl. That's why they made a good team. Doogie supplied the girls and Popmaster supplied the heroin.

They both had the perfect place to enjoy both. Sometimes they had to fight for their territory when another group of drug heads wanted to take over their place, but that was no problem for Popmaster. He always won.

Speaking of their territory, Doogie glanced toward the large building still several feet away. "Man, I don't know what Bang was shooting up when he called me earlier and said someone had locked the door. It was some good shit, whatever it was. That door is never locked."

"He could've shared with us." Popmaster whined and squeezed his girl to his side.

Reaching the front entrance of the old abandoned manufacturing warehouse, Doogie blinked several times. "What the hell?" He closed his eyes and opened them again. He shook his head to clear his fogged brain. His flashlight wavered. His arm dropped from the fiery red-head as he glanced at Popmaster with raised brows. Confused, he looked back at the building and scratched his head.

Popmaster stared at the lock and stated the obvious. "Yeah, man. What the hell? The door's got a lock on it. Bang wasn't lying." He jerked the lock several times in case he was hallucinating. But, the lock was real. He staggered to the side in disbelief. "Holy crap, man. Someone has locked us out of our Penthouse suite. What're we going to do now, Doogie? My babe isn't happy."

"Hell, I don't know. Let me think." Doogie wasn't willing to give up his playhouse. His girl nuzzled against him, her breasts rubbed against him. Her mouth sucked his earlobe. "Maybe there's another way in." He shined his light beam upwards. The only thing his flashlight uncovered was metal siding above the double doors going to the roof.

Then, out of the eerie darkness they heard several raised and unfamiliar, female voices. "Help. Help us. We've been kidnapped."

"What the hell?" The four slid on the gravel as they ran backwards. Doogie landed on one knee, his girl went with him. Popmaster regained his balance and bent to help them up. His whole body shook.

Finally standing, they heard loud, frantic calls. "Please, call the police. Help. Are you still there. Please, help us. Help."

Popmaster twirled on his feet, his wide-eyes pierced through the darkness. His knees shook. "Holy shit, man. This is like a bad, horror flick. Someone's going to be killed. Let's get the hell out of here before something bad happens."

Doogie backed away from the warehouse, his head nodding up and down in agreement. Then, back and forth. "No, man. We've got to help 'em. But, there's no way in hell we can get inside with that lock on there. You're right. Let's go."

The four ran at a staggering, fast pace back to the vehicle. The girlfriend's frantic screams of ax murderers killing them were deafening in the night's stillness.

Inside the car, Doogie fumbled the keys and dropped them. They landed on the floorboard and skidded beneath the seat. Groping in the darkness, he found the key and managed to insert it into the ignition and start the car. They took off with squealing tires.

Moments later, after only meeting one vehicle on the single lane road, Doogie pulled off to the side and onto the gravel. His hands shook as he dialed 911.

CHAPTER TWENTY SIX

Immediately after the call came in Chief Haynes tracked Dobbs and Jackson outside of the Jones' home. "We have an anonymous caller. Some guy is adamant he heard several females screaming for help inside an abandoned warehouse out on Old Industrial Loop. He says there's a new padlock on the outside of the door. He'd been there many times in the past and it had never been locked before. I figure it's one of the many drug addicts using the place frequently as a hideout to party and get high. We've found paraphernalia in there before. I need you and Jackson to check it out in case it is Woods and the girls. It's worth a shot."

Adrenaline pumped through Dobbs. "Yes, Sir. I know the place. We can be there in thirty."

* * *

Tara shot straight up. She heard a vehicle's motor for the third time. She was almost too exhausted and disheartened to care anymore. Her hopes had risen and fallen too many times in the past few hours.

But, as soon as she heard the door slam she rallied and began screaming for help. "I don't know who you are, but please, please…..,please don't leave us. I'm Detective Woods and I have the two missing girls with me. We have been kidnapped. I'm begging you to help us. If you don't call the police for us, he will kill us." The girls joined in pleading for help.

Tara took in a sharp breath. She heard the crunch of footsteps getting closer. Her hopes began to rise, again. "Please, help us."

Suddenly the large door began to slide upwards. And, there stood their kidnapper in the doorway. The moonlight threw his tall shadow against the wall. "Surprise."

He swept his flashlight across the immense room taking in the three of them still bound and scared. His sinister laugh caused a cold chill to run down her spine.

He walked further into the room. "Now, you didn't think I would stay away long enough for someone else to find you, did you?" He pulled a key out of his pocket and unlocked Candace's chain. He pulled the metal off and jerked her to her feet. She screamed.

Tara struggled against her chains. "Leave her alone. Why are you doing this?"

Candace jerked away, but he grabbed her and held on tight. His flashlight jerked upwards and his face was illuminated.

Tara gasped as she looked into familiar eyes, yet sinister this time. "You. You're the dog walker I see every morning outside my apartment."

He laughed, uncaring. "So, you recognize me. It won't do you any good where you're going." He pushed Candace out the door. A few minutes later, he returned for Jenny.

Jenny fought until he back-handed her. Throwing his stunned victim over his shoulder, he once again went outside.

Tara was livid. And, fearful. "You, bastard. You will pay for this," she screamed out.

Then. It was her turn. She was ready for him as soon as her lock came off. She kicked upwards from her sitting position. The ball of her foot hit squarely on his knee. He went down fast and hard. His curse echoed off the walls.

Before she could get her stiff body to move, he grabbed her ankle and pulled her forward until he was on top of her.

Her palm smashed into his nose. He yelled out and blood trickled down his face, but he held on tight. He grabbed both of her wrists and held them together. Grabbing the chain, he wrapped it around both of her wrists and clicked the lock back in place.

He cursed, stood and jerked her to her feet. Limping, he drug her kicking and screaming out the door and to a small van. He shoved her inside the small confines where he'd already chained the two girls.

His frigid glare never wavered. He pulled his revolver out of his pocket and pointed it toward Jenny. He dared Tara with a menacing grin. "Now, do something stupid, bitch. I'll kill your friend on the spot."

She seethed and kept her mouth shut while considering her options. Could she overpower him before he could pull the trigger or chain her, again? She played the scene out in her head for all of two seconds.

Before he could lock her chains, she reacted. "You son-of-a-bitch," she screamed out as the palm of her hand hit him square between his eyes and her other hand karate chopped the hand holding the gun. She heard bones breaking. She hoped his screams of agony alerted help.

But, just as swiftly, he retaliated. He backhanded her with his good hand, knocking her backwards against the floor. Her head hit hard.

Her heart sank as the cargo door snapped shut. The last conscious thought she had was, "God, help us."

CHAPTER TWENTY SEVEN

At ten o'clock, twenty-five long minutes after the call came through, Dobbs and Jackson arrived at the old abandoned warehouse.

The car's bright lights illuminated the raised overhang doors. Dobbs' heart sank. He glanced at Jackson and knew from his expression he was thinking the same thing.

They were too late.

Exiting from the car, they drew their pistols and shined their flashlights as they approached the building with trained caution. Adrenalin pumped through Dobbs' veins. He didn't know what they would find inside the darkened and vacant building.

Each took an opposite side of the two slide up doors. Swinging their guns in front of them they swiveled toward the entrance and surveyed the inside. Would they find Tara and the girls dead? Dobbs' gun hand shook.

They saw no one.

Giving an all clear to Jackson, they rushed the room. With their guns raised, they cleared both the downstairs and upstairs rooms within minutes.

The building was empty.

Downstairs they discovered the three sets of dog bowls placed along the wall. Large, closed hooks, the same as in Jones' home were screwed into massive beams used to hook the chains together.

Anger boiled inside Dobbs. They had to've missed them by mere minutes. How did they not meet them on the mile-long, two lane road going to the building?

He twirled on his feet, wanting to destroy the place. Wanting to take his guilt and frustrations out on something. As well as himself.

Dobbs knew Jackson watched him close, his clenched jaw set in stone. He put a restraining hand on Dobbs' arm. "Don't Dobbs. You don't want to destroy our only evidence. And man, don't beat yourself up. You're doing everything you can."

Dobbs took several gulping breaths before he nodded. "I know. I'm okay. I keep thinking if I had driven faster or called in backup who might have been closer and would've arrived sooner, we would've caught the bastard."

Jackson pulled up on his belt loops and gave Dobbs a stern look. "Well, dammit boy. I'm feeling the same guilt, but it's not helping Tara and those girls."

Dobbs glanced away, feeling a much needed sting of a kick in the butt. Jackson was right. He had to get his mind back on the game.

He looked around the room and then down to his watch. "It's 9:30. They couldn't have been gone but a few minutes when we arrived. Jones had to have arrived right after we got the call. It would have taken him time to load the three up in his van and leave before we met them on the road."

He patted Jackson on the shoulder and returned his pistol to its holder. "I need to call Chief Haynes. Then, let's go find Tara and the girls."

* * *

Doogie and the other three passengers had come back down off their high. Shitless fear would bring you down faster than you can say, "I'm screwed."

He knew what he had to do. He might stay high most of the time, but his mama had taught him right from wrong. And, he knew in his gut that this was all wrong. Those girls in the warehouse were in danger. He remembered hearing something on the radio about some teenage girls who went to school a district over being kidnapped. He wondered if that were them held in the warehouse.

He turned his head toward the backseat and nodded at Popmaster, who nodded back with a quick jerk of his head. He gave his whimpering red-head a soothing squeeze. Their minds were completely made up.

Doogie gave the white van a few seconds to get out of sight before pulling off the hidden side-road. He followed at a safe distance.

CHAPTER TWENTY-EIGHT

Tara slowly regained consciousness. Her head pounded from the head butt against the cargo floor. Opening her eyes she saw Jenny and Candace leaning against each other. Both girls comforted the other as they quietly shed tears. Their heavy chains were locked tight inside the cargo space. He wasn't taking any chances they would escape.

Tara pushed herself up until her back rested against the cargo wall. She would've loved a good bawling fit herself, but she needed to stay strong for them. She'd momentarily given up the fight when they were in the warehouse. But, now she had to rally herself and the girls to fight for their lives.

She whispered softly to calm the girls hoping he wouldn't hear her over the radio from the front seat. "Girls, are you okay?"

Jenny raised up, her eyes widened and her body quivered. "Thank God, you're alive. You were so still we thought you might be dead. We couldn't tell."

Her split lip had crusty blood caked on one corner and burned like crazy from his backhand slap. She figured she looked much worse than she felt. "I'm okay. I need you two to stay strong for me so we can focus on getting away from him. Any opportunity given, we have to take. Understand?"

They both nodded. "I don't want to die, Tara," Jenny said, heaving tears clogging her throat, once more.

The pain in her voice went straight to Tara's heart. She couldn't physically comfort her. All she could do was take a deep breath and appear confident in front of them. She couldn't let them see her fears. False hope was all she could give them. "I won't let that happen, Jenny. We'll get out of this and that monster will get what he deserves. You have to trust me."

Jenny nodded. "I'm trying."

"I know sweetheart. Try to get some rest. You too, Candace. We will need all of our sharp wits later."

Then, the radio went silent and she heard him mumbling to himself in the driver's seat as he drove them to what could be their final destination.

* * *

Long minutes later, the van slowed to a stop. The motor went silent. Tara prepared herself.

The back cargo door opened with a jerk. He stood in her line of vision, a shadowy monster with the intent to kill them.

Over her dead body.

She heard water splashing against wood and smelled the pungent odor of fish and algae. She vaguely remembered the smell from her father taking her fishing off a pier about an half an hour's drive from their home. One small memory she treasured of her father when she was around seven years old. Before his death.

But, she didn't have time to reflect on her father. It was detriment to their survival that she concentrated on her line of defense. Time was running out.

How can things happen so fast yet, seem to move in slow motion, she wondered as Jenny, the closest was yanked kicking and screaming out of the raised door first.

Tara's heart's rapid beat increased as she heard Jenny scream, a pop from a gun's silencer and a then a loud splash.

Hysterical, her heart pumping, she was helpless as the same happened to Candace. She cursed and screamed. Then, it was her turn.

He reached inside, clicked the lock open with his key and loosened the chains. They fell to the ground. His pistol wavered when he jerked her out of the door. She landed on her numb feet and fell to her knees on to pavement. She gritted her teeth, refusing to give him the satisfaction of seeing her in pain.

"Does your family know what a sick bastard you are?" Tara spat out.

He back-handed her, his face twisted in anger. His words were as hard as his fist. "Leave my family out of this. I've lost them because of your interference in my life. You should've left me alone. It's your fault that you and those girls have to die." Tears began falling down his face. "Bitch, you will never know the hell I grew up in. My alcoholic father was a bastard, but he kept my insane mother in place.

When he died...," His words broke off, his face screwed up in rage. He glanced toward the water and continued. "..., when he died she kept me chained up in our basement. She fed and watered me out of dog bowls. She kept me out of the way so she could service the long line of men coming and going. Money. She wanted their money. Bitch, do you know how horrible that was for me?"

Tara's body shook. "No. I can't imagine the horror. It doesn't have to end like this, though. I can get you some help."

He glanced back at her. His angry, blue eye pierced her to the ground. "Of course you don't know. No one does." He sighed and blew out a breath of regret. "And, I don't need your damn help. I will never be confined like that, again. I won't let you take me in."

"Think of your son and wife. What will happen to them?"

"Leave them out of this," he exploded.

In a distance, she heard sirens. He turned toward the sound, his features resigned.

Hope filled her. But, she couldn't depend on the help coming for them. While his attention was averted, she rose to her feet, twirled and kicked out, catching him in his chest. He staggered backwards a couple of feet. Before Tara could move, she watched in slow motion as he righted himself and raised his gun. She felt the sharp, intense pain from the bullet entering her upper body and knocking her off her feet. She plunged deep into the murky water.

She drifted into the darkness. Down. Down. Her lungs started to fill. Blood swirled around her. Her own blood. She kicked her body all the way around her, tangling in moss. She couldn't see the girls. Where were they?

Moments passed before her feet hit the shallow bottom of the lake allowing herself to kick herself back up toward the surface. Close to unconsciousness, she saw the two girls through the murkiness being lifted upwards out of the water. So surreal. Was she hallucinating?

Then, strong arms embraced her, lifting her to precious air. She landed softly onto the pier. Dobbs turned her onto her back and began to breathe life back into her as he pressed onto her chest.

"1...2...3," he counted out his pumps over and over until she jerked sideways and the water gushed out of her lungs. Weak and disoriented, her lashes fluttered. She took several deep breaths. Raising her head, she looked around for the girls and panicked. "Jenny? Candace? Dobbs, where are they? I saw someone lifting them up. Are they okay?"

"Shhh..., don't hurt yourself. Two young guys jumped in and rescued them. They will be okay, but they'll need medical attention The bullets just grazed both of them. Jackson is with them. The ambulance is on its way. Now, you're a different story. I need you to lie still. You've lost a lot of blood."

She felt the lethargic weakness drifting down her body. She couldn't keep her eyes open and concentrate on what Dobbs was telling her. She felt it was important and she needed to tell him something. "He lives about two blocks over. I don't know his name. Dog."

Dobbs sat back on his heels. "Albert Jones was his name. He's dead. The last bullet in his gun's chamber went through his own skull, as he intended. Young girls are safe from him from now on. So are you."

Tara gulped a sob of major relief. He was dead. Jenny and Candace was safe.

And, she hurt like hell.

When the paramedics arrived, Tara was amazed that one of them was the same guy who had treated her a couple days before.

"We've got to quit meeting like this, Detective." The paramedic grinned and helped his partner lift her onto the stretcher.

Tara grimaced. "I agree."

Dobbs held her hand all of the way to the ambulance where Jenny and Candace were being treated.

Tara and the girls hugged and held on to each other, sobs of relief flowed between them.

CHAPTER TWENTY NINE

Bloody hell, she hurt. Sometime Thursday morning, Tara forced her eyes open and saw stark white walls and a nurse standing by her bed holding a clipboard. Jake stood beside the nurse, carefully touching Tara's hand that held an IV needle inserted and taped to the top. He grinned down at her and leaned down to kiss her on her forehead. "You're awake. Thank God, Baby. I was so worried. How are you feeling?"

Tara licked her dry lips and her words came out no more than a weak whisper. "Like I was run over by a semi." She heard a chuckle from her other side and carefully turned her head to see Dobbs standing on the other side of her bed with Jenny and Stacy standing beside him. Dobbs' parents, Jackson and Chief Haynes stood behind them. She noticed Candace, wearing an arm sling and her parents were standing outside her room along with two teenage boys she'd never met before. Candace and Jenny seemed to be okay despite their ordeal.

Jenny, with one arm swathed in bandages moved closer and gently hugged her, tears of gratitude streamed down her face. Stacy moved beside her and spoke. "Other than your three broken ribs, a bullet hole in your upper arm, and have a slight concussion, you a huge knot on your head.

The doctor wants to monitor you today and tonight. He said you could go home tomorrow if you don't develop any other complications."

"Thanks. That's the best news I've heard in days." She wanted to be home and in her own bed with Jake by her side to lick her wounds.

Stacy wrapped her arm around her daughter, holding her close. "I know you need to rest and Nurse Bennett is giving us the evil eye because you have a room full of visitors when it's way past visiting hours, so we won't stay long. Jenny and Candace wouldn't leave until they were sure you were okay. I wanted to thank you for everything you've done. How can I ever repay you for saving my Jenny?"

Tara grimaced from the physical and mental anguish. "By forgiving me for getting her in the mess in the first place." Would she ever be able to forgive herself for the suffering her loved ones went through?

"I never blamed you. How could you ever know what that pervert would do? He has paid the ultimate price for what he's done to those other girls and what he would've done to Jenny if you hadn't been there."

Tara smiled grimly up at Jenny and Stacy. She pushed the loose strand of hair from Jenny's forehead. "I'm so glad you're okay, sweetheart. You were so brave. I don't know what I would've done if he'd hurt you or Candace." She glanced over at Dobbs. "I want a full report."

Jake's stern voice interrupted. "It's six a.m., Tara. You need to get some rest. They can tell you everything this evening after you've had hours of bed rest and feel better."

Tara glared up at Jake. He was usually very good at knowing exactly what she needed and wanted. But, not this time. "How can I get any rest without knowing what happened? Dobbs. Report to me, now."

Jake raised his hand in surrender. "Okay, but I insist you get some rest later. If everyone doesn't mind leaving and coming back later, I would appreciate it."

Tara had to wait until everyone filed out of her room, except Jake, Dobbs, Chief Haynes and Jackson. They remained behind to fill her in.

Dobbs grinned and reached for her other hand when Jake stepped back. "Of course, but first I want you to meet your rescuers." He motioned for the two boys still standing in the hallway to come to her bedside. "Tara, this is John, aka Doogie and this big guy here is Mark, aka Popmaster. They are the ones who heard you screaming for help in the warehouse and called 911. Then, they followed Jones to the pier where they called in again to lead us to you and the girls. They dived in and pulled Jenny and Candace to the surface. If it weren't for them, we wouldn't be talking to you or the girls, right now."

Tara reached out her good hand and squeezed each boy's hand in turn. "I don't know how to thank you two. You saved our lives."

"It was nothing, ma'am. I'm just glad we showed up when we did," Doogie told her.

Tara smiled wryly. "Me too. We owe you our lives. Thank you."

"No problem, Detective." Doogie shuffled on his feet and glanced toward the door. "Well, I guess we'll be on our way so you can get some rest. We just wanted to make sure you and the girls were okay. If you don't mind, we'll stop by this evening in case Jenny and Candace drops by to check on you. We want to make sure they're still doing okay. Oh, and to check on you too, of course."

Popmaster smiled and nodded. "Yeah. I get off work around six tonight. We can come after that if it's okay with you."

This time, Tara grinned. The two boys obviously had an interest in the girls. "We would love to see you. I'm sure the girls will want to personally thank you for jumping in and rescuing them. And, thank you both." Tara knew what those boys had been up to at the warehouse earlier, but she also sensed they were trustworthy. That didn't mean she or Stacy would want the girls to be alone with them.

Dobbs turned to Tara after the boys left. "One other thing. With Chief Haynes' permission, I asked our divers to search beneath the pier early this morning while searching for Jones. His body was lying against the bank a few yards down. While searching, the divers found several skeletons, possibly thirty or more lying on the bottom. All females."

"Oh my, God. How? What else?" Tara stumbled over her words. Her hand covered her mouth in shock.

Dobbs rested a hand on her shoulder. "Crude cement blocks were tied around their waists taking them to their final resting place. The divers are bringing them up, one by one. Forensic is busy trying to identify the remains, one by one."

Tara's tired brain tried to take in all of the information Dobbs gave her. Something wasn't clicking for her. She glanced from Dobbs to Chief Haynes and Jackson. "Could they tell by the bones if the girls beneath the pier had been mutilated in any way?"

"The ones pulled up so far had a bullet hole in their skull, but no obvious mutilation," Jackson told her.

"So, why would he shoot and dump some girls in the water beneath the pier, yet leave some lying where they were killed and sliced open like someone cutting open a chicken to fry?"

Dobbs shrugged. "I don't have an answer for you on that one, but we won't stop until we find out."

Tara grinned. "Damn right, we won't. At least now, we can give their families final closure." Her eyelids grew heavy and her thoughts fuzzy. She finally felt safe and wished she could take whatever kind of pain medicine they were giving her in her IV home with her tomorrow. Home. God, she loved that word.

Raising her eyelids she glanced over at Jake, her dark-haired Adonis holding her right hand, her lover, her friend. A man she wanted in her life forever, who would provide for her. Love her, treat her like a lady. Be beside her when she needed him the most. Have a cold beer and a warm bath waiting on her at two o'clock in the morning. With the best sex ever afterwards.

And, then she turned to her left and gazed at Dobbs, sexy, blonde, kickass, bad boy still clasping her other hand, her partner, her friend. Someone who always had her back, one she could always depend on, trust. A man she could laugh with, tease and would make her welcome in a bar surrounded by the 'boys' from their precinct. Kinda like a brother, she realized.

Jake, Dobbs, Stacy, Jenny, Jackson and Chief Haynes made up her family, now. And, she was loved.

With that last thought, her eyes relaxed and fluttered closed as the medicine worked its magic.

EPILOGUE

Little Timmy removed his hands from around her neck and softly, sensually caressed the new girl's ghostly, pale face. He kissed her once more before closing her pale eyelids. She could no longer see out of those beautiful, green eyes.

He stood and zipped up his pants, mourning the fact he would have to continue his dad's legacy alone. But, he'd been doing it alone for a long while without his Dad's knowledge. It was a thrill he couldn't live without.

Little Timmy pulled out his fillet knife and went to work.

This was his legacy, his heredity. The only thing he had left of his father.

His deceased father. He was dead because of Detective Tara Woods and Detective Matt Dobbs.

Someday, revenge would be his.

The next 'Tara' stand alone series.

TERRORIZING TARA

Tree branches slapped the young woman's face as she ran deeper into the forest during the darkest of night. Deep, blubbering sobs racked her body covering the sound of footsteps pounding the ground behind her.

Glancing back for a fatal instant, she didn't see the fallen log in front of her. Until, it was too late. She tripped, landed hard on her stomach knocking the breath out of her. The panic rushing inside her seized her heartbeat and slammed it hard against her chest. Please, God. Please, please God.

Wiping her tangled hair from the wetness of tears mingled with the fresh blood and dirt on her face, the woman rose to her feet and began running for her life. Her legs trembled and she staggered and weaved her way toward freedom, away from the two day unbearable nightmare she'd endured, suffered and finally escaped.

And, then hands came out of the darkness and grabbed her.

Connect with JERI LYNN STONE

I really appreciate you reading my books! I would love to hear from you. I appreciate all of my fans. I write for you and for my sanity.

If you enjoyed reading Tangle with Tara

please leave an honest review on Amazon.

Here are my social media coordinates:

Friend me on Facebook:
http://facebook.com/jerilynnstone
Follow me on Twitter:
http://twitter.com/jerlynstone
Subscribe to my blog:
http://www.jerilynnstone.blogspot.com

TANGLE WITH TARA

www.ingramcontent.com/pod-product-compliance
Lightning Source LLC
Chambersburg PA
CBHW021430110726
47901CB00008B/2375